OF UNSEEN THINGS ABOVE

MYRNA BROWN

FriesenPress

Suite 300 - 990 Fort St
Victoria, BC, Canada, V8V 3K2
www.friesenpress.com

Copyright © 2015 by Myrna Brown
First Edition — 2015

All rights reserved.

ISBN
978-1-4602-6820-9 (Hardcover)
978-1-4602-6821-6 (Paperback)
978-1-4602-6822-3 (eBook)

1. Fiction, Romance

Distributed to the trade by The Ingram Book Company

DEDICATION

Denis Brown. It is out of our love this book was born.

Peda peda pamda la
pedaba ka pam ye
Some are receiving, but
others do not receive

A DOORWAY

She stands in the doorway, a gray metal door, louvered to block the sun, so warm that she releases the handle quickly. She faces north in a shaft of late afternoon light from an ocean of sky, and sees a roiling wave of dust mounting, a hazy pillar sweeping toward her from the red earth's scrub, the sun bleached grass-lands that stretch to the edges of the Sahara desert. It is March, and the cruel season of the harmattan trade winds is nearly over.

Almost a year since her ordination, she has come to live among the Mossi tribe, farmers of this sub-Sahel savannah, the largest ethnic group in land-bound La Haute Volta.★

She smells the damp, dusty air that sweeps through before a storm, familiar to her now. Stepping inside, she quickly closes the metal glassless windows, lightly feeling the heat in the tips of her fingers.

In the dim light, she follows the white-washed walls to the kitchen, simply constructed of planks placed atop her packing barrels with a two kerosene burner stove and a cranky kerosene

---

★ Now Burkina Faso

refrigerator. She draws a protective cloth over the orange and yellow ripening mangos. The two kerosene burners are in use roasting a guinea fowl and blanching the green beans Boukari, the yard man, has found in the market that morning.

Rattling the metal windows, the northeast trade wind escorts the sandy dust billowing off the plain through the louvers, beneath the doors, filling her nostrils, the dankness competing with the browning chicken and the earthy green smell of the beans. She adjusts the knobs of the burners, trying to get a blue, steady flame.

On the skirts of the dust, the rain follows. It drums on the tin roof like a large and pleased audience, torrential, reaching a deafening crescendo; letting up; spattering without rhythm and suddenly stopping. The winds pass, continuing a route to New Guinea leaving the air heavy and cooler. It smells of wet clay. The silence, the solitude, and separation are tangible like the weighted air.

She hears voices and laughter, and she reopens the louvers, blinking against the returned light. A pale green gecko runs up the grill past her hand. Through a curtain of ascending vapor she sees several men gathered on the muddied path to the market. They've stood out under the deluge celebrating and soaking up the end of a long drought. Bending over, she loosens and shakes her hair, rearranges it off her neck and steps outside, relieved by their presence, the sound of their run-together syllables. She turns her nose to the sky; breathes the freshened air and laughing with them, she spreads her arms saying, "*Ya Wennam bosego!*" It's God's blessing.

"*Baraka Wennam,*" they chime, thank God. Augustin, her landlord and first friend, a widowed Mossi physician who manages the local clinic, is with them, sitting on his dull blue, scarred-up Vespa, one hand on his hip, leg extended, drenched. She meets his gaze and gestures to the zandi.

Their laughter is as refreshing as the rain. Small steaming mud puddles quiver, sparkling, overflowing, trickling as they wash over the path. In their white, loose-fitting short trousers and their open flowing shirts sagging on their shoulders they huddle, skull caps in hand. The clouds have passed with the wind, and the sun is hot. The rain evaporates in foggy tendrils, escaping the crenellated, sunbaked soil.

Augustin dismounts and grasps one of the twisted poles bearing the weight of the newly constructed zandi as if testing it, laughingly shaking the rain in sheets onto the floor of red clay. He watches Thea's face as if he is curious about this tall, fair blonde come from America to challenge the beliefs of a whole people, Muslims and Animists alike. Her hands fly to cover her head.

He stoops and runs his broad hand over the smooth shine of the clay floor, the newly pounded zekka. The red laterite rock of which it has been made is dug up and pounded until it is as glossy as the glazed clay of the Mossi pots, the specialty of one of the many castes.

Augustin's hands are broad with long fingers. She sees some engendered gentleness in them, a capacity for kindness. She sees the lighter underside of his palm, seamed with darker lines. He is composed again, but the permanent lines on his face tell of his compassion.

He seems impressed by the zandi. He nods approvingly, glancing her way. "*Ne pongo*,"congratulations, he says. "So the Kaya Christians have built this for you?"

He steps toward her, and the other faces are lost to her. Their chatter goes on as they too admire the zekka and stroke the crooked poles holding up the zandi.

She nods. The zandi is a gift from the Christians in the next village of Kaya. They built it soon after she came. She knows they want her to plant a new church here beneath the zandi, even though they haven't told her as much. The Swiss Protestants in

Ouagadougou, who had helped Thea locate in Kongoussi, tell her of the vibrant congregation in the village of Kaya, an old village, situated on an ancient trade route, one of the routes that leads to Timbuktu in the dry season. The Kaya leader, Pastor Barri, well known for his gift of healing by laying on of hands, is extremely zealous and wants to plant new churches in the surrounding villages, Kongoussi included. He delegates and encourages those members willing to walk the distance to build the zandi and pound the zekka in the compound of the new missionary from America.

Prior to the zandi being built, a small group from the church in Kaya has walked the ten kilometers to bring her gifts: a sheaf of millet, an enameled pan full of guinea fowl eggs, and hand-made balls of mottled green soap.

One of the Kaya visitors speaks French and explains to her about the gift of the zandi.

"Mademoiselle, you won't have any shade unless we build you a grass shelter."

"I completely agree," Thea says.

Then, day after day, they come to build it. Each day, she makes grape, sugar-free Kool-Aid that her mother sends in petite pac-quets. She pours it, the color of weak wine, into glasses, using them all. It works a kind of miracle, and the workers hold them to the sun and turn them around, the pleasure reflected in their faces.

To build it, the visiting Christians come dragging the scarce, long, crooked poles they find in the bush. They dig the postholes in the hard red clay, taking turns breaking the sod with an ax. After the straw thatch roof is woven, the women begin pound-ing a floor. Over several days, they bend from the waist down, singing and pounding in rhythm. Captivated and feeling she has guests, Thea stirs up more of the much-loved grape Kool-Aid.

The evening the women finish pounding the red clay to a smooth sheen, tambourines appear, and they dance and sing in graceful rhythm. Bare breasted, bare footed, wearing woven cloth wrappers around their hips and legs, they prance playfully on the smooth cool surface. On their left arms they wear jangling brass bracelets. Thea brings out the kerosene lamps so the night can continue, kicks off her sandals, and joins them in their dance, wanting their company, trying to follow their steps. They clap and lean into themselves in laughter. "My mother didn't teach me," Thea explains out of breath.

Now, still celebrating the first rain of the season under the freshly built zandi with her neighbors, the zandi smells of the newly harvested grass made more pungent by the rain.

The men who had come begin to go their separate ways. "*Ne Zabri*," they call the evening greeting as they leave single file.

"*Ne Zabri*," Good evening, she calls back, still testing the Moore words on her tongue. West African French has come easier than Moore, the Mossis' language.

NEW LEGENDS

Augustin is seated once again astride his Vespa, his hand on the ignition. He alone wears western clothes. Even as soaked as he is, she can see the pleats in the back of his shirt have been pressed.

Augustin doesn't turn the motor, he asks, "Did you like the sound of the rain on the roof?"

"It reminded me of a concert, perhaps Vivaldi's Summer."

"The soft rains will put you to sleep."

The home she has rented from Augustin is new, the only cement block house in the village and has the only corrugated aluminum roof. He owns a Peugeot, one of the few vehicles in the community. Checking on his property and Thea, his first tenant, he often stops in late afternoon after he has finished his day at the clinic.

Daily, he sees the patients at the clinic waiting in two slow-moving lines, the first to give their name and approximate date of birth to the aide, the other to be treated. Forming queues, they curl around the building, crowding against the white-washed walls to find shade, coming with a variety of illnesses:

malaria, dysentery, micro filaria, fever and coughs, a new unnamed disease the Africans have dubbed "slim."

The clinic has a driver, Simon, who waits about, leaning against the ancient Deux Cheveaux, the clinic's car called a *mobile*. The two cylinder vehicle is parked ready to take those too sick to be treated in Kongoussi to the hospital in Ouagadougou, a dusty hour and a half away due south on a rutted dirt road. Washboard," they call it. The harsh shifting of gears as the mobili pulls onto the road reminds her of Betsy, the old Massey Ferguson tractor back home, a corroded and tired-orange brute still up to the task.

"I was just dropping by to check on you. Hopefully, the roof didn't leak." Augustin says.

She shakes her head. "You've finished at the clinic then? I'm glad you're here. I really need some advice."

He dismounts easily, walking with a slight limp, like Jacob of old, who wrestled with the angel. His name recalls St. Augustine, an important Church Father in Western Christianity, recognized since the fourth century. He believed the grace of Christ was indispensable. But there is no Christ as Savior for Augustin. He is Muslim. Still soaked through, he sits with her under the zandi in one of the two complaining folding chairs.

Thea corrects the strap of her bra and crosses her legs. Leaning forward, her chair creaks, the dry wood resisting her movement.

"Augustin, before I tell you what's concerning me, I have a question . . . from what I know, much of the history of the Mossis has never been written. Except for a few recent French anthropologists, so little has been recorded about the tribe. I just wonder about their past compared to the present. Is their history really an oral one?"

Augustin straightens in his chair and rubs his chin. He seems to brighten as if he welcomes the subject. "At one time, we were a much bigger tribe and dominated most of the sub Sahel. All of our history and traditions come down through stories and legends. The details are dependent on memory. Even now new legends are incorporated, like stories and lessons learned from this extended drought. I pass on the stories told to me to my sons just as my father did."

"What a beautiful tradition. Your sons are able to know you then, in the context of your own history."

"There was a lot of change when the Europeans came, not just here but in all of Africa. It's harder and harder to hold onto the old ways."

"But you're here, doing that, even after studying medicine at the Sorbonne."

"My sons and their children are here. This is home."

"I've read about how the Belgians exploited the Congo during the times of King Leopold especially. I originally wanted to go to Stanleyville in the Congo, but this was the only opportunity that came up."

"Before you know it, it will feel like home.

The Mossis cherished their independence and were one of the last tribes in Africa to be colonized.

Even now they hold on to much of their culture: the Mogho Naaba, the king, and the chiefs beneath him with their royal dress and regalia. The French established a government here in 1896, but La Haute Volta struggled and did not become an autonomous republic in the French community until December of 1960. French by then had been established as the official language.

My lineage is that of the Mogho Naba, chiefs and aristocrats, men who rode in the cavalry. The villagers expect a lot of me because of that. They know I'm here because I want to protect our lifestyle, as incongruous as it may seem to the Europeans. My dream is to see health and education provided to girls and boys alike while maintaining our customs and way of life."

"I can see how you're respected by the villagers; even by the way they greet you."

Thea tries to see the village through his eyes, having seen the inequities in contrast to the beauty of the way of life, a cadence she finds soothing. She sees the intensity in his eyes.

"Right now I'm in a quandary . . .

A Fulani comes to my door every day asking me to buy the milk she brings in a calabash atop her head. When I refuse, she turns and shows me the infant on her back. The baby is starving. She lifts her sagging breasts, which are obviously empty, and shakes her head, telling me she can't feed her baby. She seems to be asking for my help though I know from my reading that by tradition the Fulanis don't ask for help outside their tribe."

She is drawn to his capable hands, the left cradling the right as he rubs the thumb and forefinger together. Augustin responds, "She's one of the Fulanis driven south during this drought away from their usual pasture routes and water holes, some here to Kongoussi."

"Why to this particular village?"

"We've the only lake available within kilometers of desert to water their cattle, and the Mossis tolerate them better here than in other villages."

"How do they subsist?"

"They're trading their prized breeding stock in the market at cheap prices just to eat. They live primarily on the milk products. Many of the cows have stopped producing. I don't think they would ask a Mossi for help, let alone you, such a stranger. I'm surprised, Thea."

She considers this without commenting. She has noticed the Fulani "bukkaru" shelters are much different from the Mossis' homes. The people, too, are distinguishable and don't mix with the Mossis. Their domed portable houses are encamped around the village. At nightfall their fires flicker and lick the flat horizon. The jagged strand of ruby embers lasts long into the night.

The Fulanis can see the lone white cement block house in which she lives, sitting on a slight knoll, surrounded by the round, mud brick, thatched *dogos* of the Mossis. In contrast, the easily moved *bukkaru* of the Fulanis are supported merely by millet stalk pillars and reed mats tied together while the Mossi homes are built to last. Facing west, the round Mossi *dogos* have thick red mud walls that stay cool during the day and trap the heat during the night.

Fulani men in their conical leather hats, their colorful, often striped robes, hold their walking sticks across their shoulders with their arms resting on top and take the path in front of her home. Their Zebu cattle have muddied the shoreline of the small shrunken lake she can see in the distance. The Fulani women are tall compared to Mossi women and are very fine featured.

"Do the Fulanis come to your clinic?" she asks.

Augustin shifts in his chair and runs his long fingers along the line of his chin. "I've never treated a Fulani. They rarely mingle, let alone come to a government sponsored clinic."

"Is there competition between the tribes for the land during droughts like this?"

"I have to say an emphatic 'yes' to that question. They don't recognize the governments or borders of other countries, let alone those of individuals. The Mossis are concerned for their millet fields. Rightly so. Raising cattle and raising millet on the same land is impossible. They're not very welcome, and they know it. But they keep apart. If the rains come soon enough and the Fulanis clear out of the village, planting can get started, and there'll be less tension. The desert is getting larger all the time so who knows how their tribe will be affected in generations to come?"

"No long-term solutions then?"

In the distance, Thea and Augustin hear the Muslim evening call to prayer. The red sun slips away, a sanguineous gash, bleeding into the horizon. Darkness surrounds them, and the night sounds take up the space between them.

The donkeys who have worked hard all day begin to bray, achingly, back and forth, as if calling and answering each other. She hears the voices of her neighbors around their fires. The tiny hanging bats in their mango trees squeak incessantly, sounding like sneakers on a basketball court. A Basenji, one of the singing dogs, howls its quavering song, and another begins. Thea brings a lantern. They sit quietly in comfortable silence.

Augustin, partially in shadow, leans forward, his fingers laced to cup his knees. He clears his throat and suggests, "I think that you could begin by buying the Fulani milk. Sterilize it, add sugar, then talk to the mother about force feeding the baby drop by drop until the baby's appetite returns.

The babies become anorexic; the appetite just finally goes away after not having any nutrition for a long period . . . a condition called Kwashiorkor . . . You'd have to repeat the process every four hours. In time, the appetite should return. It would require quite a commitment on your part. If you succeed, there will be more infants . . ." Augustin shifts in his chair and leaves his sentence unfinished.

"I've heard of Kwashiorkor but never witnessed it until the Fulani woman came. I'll need an interpreter," she says. "I don't know a single word of Fulfulde."

Before her is an obligation to help a starving infant, no matter how many others or which tribe or whose customs prevail.

"I came to build a church here," she continues "And I meant to minister to the Mossis, not the Fulanis."

Each afternoon she is tutored by a Mossi, using French that she has studied over five years. The little Moore she knows now won't help her with the Fulani's language. Hopefully, someone can be found who can translate directly from French to Fulfulde.

She believes the calling she had as a child has brought her here to fulfill the mission of founding a church. She believes the only way to have eternal life is through accepting Jesus Christ as Savior.

"There is no written Fulfulde," Augustin continues. "Sometimes researchers have written a few words phonetically but it will be hard to learn. Moore has only had orthography for fifty years and not much beside the Bible. . . actually, only the New Testament, and that thanks to the Protestants, has been printed. They used mimeograph machines in the beginning. You remember the importance of not making a mistake on a carbon copy."

"Oh, my gosh, do I remember? All those papers I wrote . . ."

"The Evangelicals have a unique concept in direct contrast to the government's approach to literacy. They're teaching those Mossis who speak no French to read in their *own* language, first, and then move forward in French."

"The Christians are excited to become literate in Moore and French. Few of the children have been to public school, which usually don't exist here in the bush. The Evangelicals have built more schools than the government. They draw the youth who have the energy and determination for change." Augustin says, seemingly off on a tangent. He hesitates as if his thoughts have gone elsewhere. "I think I know of someone who can help with the translation."

They stand, and Thea notices his shirt has dried except in the seams. She scrunches her shoulders, shivering, and wraps her arms around herself. They can hear Boukari at the well, drawing the last bucket of rust-colored water for the day. It splashes as he pours it into the holding tank where the silt can settle before he draws it again. Her thoughts follow Augustin as the sputtering of his Vespa fades. She carries the lantern in, reluctant to leave the fineness of the night. The reflection of the orange sheen off the smooth zekka reminds her of the many kindnesses extended to her and the task ahead.

As he leaves, Thea shrinks further into herself longing for something familiar. Although she'll not return to the home of

her parents to live, she thinks of it as a refuge. Her church was
her second home.

AN EMPTY ALTAR

Reverend Greenberg, a missionary from Stanleyville, the teeming capital of the Congo, with his sermon about those who would perish without hearing the gospel and his carousel of slides, had changed the course of her life when she was six. With the lights still dim, at the end of the slide presentation, he had left on the screen an unsettling scarlet sunset, the perfect metaphor. "Soon the day of harvest will be over . . ." he quoted from a hymn. He had spoken in a lowered, quiet voice, asking for support so he and his family could take the Gospel back to the very heart of dark Africa to those who might never hear of it and could otherwise perish for eternity.

With all heads bowed as he had instructed, he had appealed to young and old to be completely committed. "Maybe God is calling someone, just as he called Samuel in his sleep. He may want to put a call on your life."

Flora, the soloist, slipped in behind the pulpit while he went down to the altar to receive and lay hands on those who felt called.

Hear the Lord of harvest sweetly calling,
"Who will go and work for me today?
Who will bring to me the lost and dying?
Who will point them to the narrow way?"
Speak my Lord, speak my Lord.
Speak and I'll be quick to answer Thee.
Speak my Lord, speak my Lord.
Speak and I will answer, "Lord send me."

When he had asked for a raise of hands from those willing to reap the harvest, to bring in the sheaves, Thea had raised her small hand and walked down the aisle to the altar, wooed by the minister and the music, but more, she felt she had found a way to have the purported personal relationship with God.

The missionary had put both hands on her head and prayed over her. She felt sure she had been called, and tears wet her cheeks as he prayed. That was the evening of her calling, a calling she professed throughout her childhood, the calling that brought her here to Kongoussi.

Now in Kongoussi, she is taken back by the hardships, but she fixes a pillow beside her bed on the concrete floor and prays for strength and grace. Every morning she kneels there. She reads and prays. She also talks to herself, reminding herself unlike Pascal that she has not taken a vow of poverty and penance. Unlike the Fulanis, she is not locked into a lifestyle of doing without.

She means to return to her abundant life left behind. She means to leave here enriched of soul, stronger in her faith. She means to leave a legacy of love reinforced and carried on by the converts among the Mossis. When finished with her mission here, she should be ready, she thinks, for her next assignment to a church by her organization. She means to move on. However, something stronger is holding her here. She feels no incentive to map her future.

UNSKIMMED MILK

The Fulani woman Thea had met returns the following morning and claps for Thea's attention at the back door to the kitchen. She lifts the calabash from atop her head and proffers the blue tinged milk that scarcely covers the bottom of the gourd. Slim and tall, her long hair has been woven into five braids, looped on the sides, plaited with silver. Her lips are stained black. Again she lifts an empty breast with her slender hand and nods to her child. The baby's hair is rusty in color, sparse and coarse, and the infant sleeps closely against its mother's back, the tiny limbs hardly bigger than wooden spatulas.

Thea receives the milk, empties the calabash, rinses it and hands the woman one hundred francs, a figure she guesses to be fair, not understanding how much money it is to the Fulani. Still holding the intricately decorated calabash against her chest, Thea points to it, indicating she would like more milk the next day. They don't speak. They resort to gestures. The Fulani shifts her baby, nods, and turns to go.

Late in the afternoon, she recognizes the sound of Augustin's Vespa before she sees it and goes to meet him beneath the zandi. Seated behind him is Norogo, a young Mossi who speaks French and Moore as well as Fulfulde. Through Norogo she will use her French to communicate with the Fulani.

Norogo is eager and shifts from one foot to another. He looks from Augustin's face to Thea's. He has the freshness of a boy, Thea thinks. She greets him with the traditional greetings, asking after his mother, his father, his brothers, his sisters. "Everything is fine," he repeats, shaking her hand after each question, "*Laafi bella*." By custom, in deference to her, he has stooped lower with each question.

Thea describes her expectations and Norogo nods, repetitively. "Everything is good then. *Wa ka ibeogo*. Come tomorrow morning. "We'll start at 6:30. How do you take your coffee?"

"Thank you, thank you. I like sweetened condensed milk with my coffee, Mademoiselle. Thank you."

He is lithe, dressed in a faded Adidas T-shirt and jeans. He leaves on foot, exiting like a dancer leaving the stage.

Thea brings glasses, and she and Augustin drink a warm Youki orange soda together, her only offering other than water. She hasn't been able to coax the kerosene refrigerator back to life. Strips of light coming through the thatch ripple across Augustin's forehead and across the zekka in the slight breeze. People call to greet him as they pass by. A translucent silence like a sheer veil separates them, something neither wants to tear or breech. She watches as he unfolds his long legs. She wants him to stay.

Unlike other compounds she has no wall. Others use her well, and there is foot traffic in front of her house throughout the day. Still, though often surrounded by people, an indescribable loneliness settles in her gut, sinking like the silt in the holding tank.

Later, with the lamp beside her, she sweats over her blue, Smith Corona portable typewriter, writing first to her parents and then to the congregation who has sponsored her. She uses erasable paper, finding it difficult to compose a description of her experience of living in a village where the drought has taken such a toll.

Dear Mother and Dad,

*I'm becoming attached here. Nothing is like I
expected. I'm being greeted everywhere I happen
to go as if I'm not a stranger. I feel very welcome.*

*I've not succeeded getting the kerosene fridge
to run. Augustin laughs at me because no one
here in Kongoussi is used to anything cold.
I don't think I'll ever adapt that much.*

*I wish I could describe the Mossis. They are such
a proud people. They still hold onto traditions that
are centuries old. Sometime when I'm walking I
come upon the remains of a sacrificed chicken or
goat. I wonder how much faith they feel as the
blood spills and they perform their rituals. The need
for faith in a higher power is universal, isn't it?*

*If not for the hardships imposed by the drought,
they are very self-sufficient. Augustin tells me
how resilient they have been, rationing their food
so they could hold on to enough to plant this
season. There are no obese among either tribe, but
the Mossis have fared better than the Fulanis.*

*In general, the Mossis I know are so good
natured. They laugh easily at themselves and
with others, like you Dad. Mother, you're
more like a Fulani, quiet and strong.*

The language is coming. I'm focusing on Moore since
only those few who've gone to school speak much
French. Translator at hand, I'm making my way.

Their main staple is Sagabo, made from the millet.
It's gritty and has no flavor except if accompanied
by a vegetable sauce. It's a bit like mush except not
as white. Their livelihood depends on the successful
harvest of the millet. Come, late autumn, hopefully,
they will have Nabasga, a celebration of the harvest.
Last year they had a pitiful harvest and had little
to celebrate. It has been very dry for a long period.

I'm intrigued by the Fulanis, how they've
come off the desert and how separate they keep.
The women stand tall and erect and walk
with a certain grace that's hard to describe.

Augustin has been such a good friend. Before I came
he had already hired Boukari who is so important
to my everyday living. Augustin has also helped
in many ways. More than just a resource he's
become a friend. I look forward to his daily visits.

I hear from Ragna often. Remember when you say
'the Lord bless you' she always responds 'He do, He
do'? She has sent wound dressings she makes from
old sheets. Her letters are a delight. In her imperfect
English, she gives me all the news, even some gossip.

You can send more of the sugar-free Kool-Aid,
particularly grape. It causes quite a stir since sugar
is only available in Ghana. If you bring it across
the border the customs are double the cost of the
sugar. It's only available in fifty pound bags. I pay
dearly for the small amounts I buy in the market.

My kitchen takes me back to our camping days.
The Swiss missionaries told me that they had
equipped it, but I had a different idea what it
would be like before I came. I've no cupboards,
but then I buy my food one day at a time . . .
I'd sure like a roll of Saran-wrap. Don't send
it! Stay within the limits of the petit pacquets
at 2 kilos, or I will have to pay customs.

I'd love to see the sunset over the river at the end
of the property. I remember it as a stretch of gold
satin, collecting all the light around it. I'd love to
see you. I remember you as steadfast and true,
collecting all the praise you do for your roles in the
church. If things were less harsh I would encourage
you to come, but I've no room for you and there's
no other place in the village you could stay.

I hope Sheila is doing better. Her baby
looks just like her, don't you think?

As you can tell, I need a new ribbon.
I'll continue this later.

Love,

Thea

Thea doesn't write about not having begun telling the
story of Jesus and his love. Presupposing the situation would
lend itself to spreading the Gospel, she is not prepared for this
village of self-sufficient people, seemingly unpoisoned by greed
or pride. Unexpectedly, they don't appear lost and 'hungry to
know God.' They seem quite happy in fact. She knows the laity
in her home church will expect to hear of the conversions of
these near 'savages'.

Distracted, she picks up one of the *Time* magazines from early April, 1972. *Vogue*, it reads, has put the first black woman on its cover. Robert Lowell's poetry has won the Pulitzer Prize. Her lips move over a memorized verse:

> *"And the candles gutter by an empty altar*
> *And land is where the bloodless land of Cain*
> *Is burning, burning the unburied grain."*

It's as if he's been here and seeing what I am seeing. She thinks of the seed that has gone unplanted thus far this season because the soil is so hardened by the perpetual sun and lack of rain. Their altars are empty because they are hungry. If sacrifice is the preface to prayer, the preparation of the heart, how sad, she thinks to have an empty altar, to be without a sacrifice.

TRIMMING THE WICK

Before noon the next day, Boukari brings home yet another guinea fowl. He draws and heats the water over an open fire made with sticks she buys from the small boys coming by her house off the savannah, leading their small, grey donkeys, burdened with stacks of lean, crooked firewood. Dusty and dragging, the boys call to her as they go by on their way to market, competing for her business. One boy breaks out of line, and she buys his whole load. Abrasions bathed in perspiration run across the donkey's back. She thinks of the Mossi proverb: "The back of a good donkey is always scraped up," the lesson being if you should go the market looking for a good donkey to hire, always check its back to see how well it works.

The dry sticks burn quickly, popping sparks that die as they descend. The flume of smoke ascends vertically in the windless midday. She is reminded of campfires in the woods at home when smoke followed beauty, and the fire was for toasting hot dogs or marshmallows, just for fun.

Boukari's back is bare and wet with perspiration. She notices his strength, the ease of movement as he swings the bucket then pumps the water through the filter. Fleetingly, she thinks of Augustin. His strength would match Boukari's, but unlike Boukari, his hands have no callouses.

She commends him on his work using the special phrase of the Mossis when they see someone working hard or well. "*Ne toum nere.*" Good work.

After Boukari has chopped off its head and the bird has stopped flopping and raising dust around the yard, she plunges it into the heated water. Momentarily, she reflects on seeing her grandmother in her usual cobbler apron wring the neck of an old layer with the turn of a wrist just outside the old chicken coop. "I can do this," she thinks as she plucks the grey wet feathers, eviscerates it and washes the musty smell off her hands.

The fowl is thin and won't be tender. Guinea fowl has become her usual fare with so little else available in the market. Eating alone, she often thinks nostalgically of food from home, the yeasty smell of baking bread or the touch of cinnamon on her toast, her mother's way of cooking venison, especially the tenderloin of a freshly killed buck surrounded by onions and apples. Later, she studies her copy of *The Joy of Cooking*, learning how to cut up a chicken or roast it whole cooktop. How would Erma Rombauer do it?

Sometimes Boukari finds guinea eggs; some are fresh; some are old or ready to hatch. She doesn't know what to expect when she cracks an egg. Because of the small size, two are needed to equal one egg at home. It usually takes four eggs, after encountering a half hatched bird or a bloody yolk. Boukari always finds a guinea fowl, green beans, tomatoes, mangos. The baguettes made in a wood fire by the baker in the market are misshapen, small and pale, hardly a reminder of a crusty French loaf. Still, they are warm when he brings them every morning.

That afternoon, lying on the floor, Thea trims the wick of the kerosene burner on the refrigerator, and it comes reluctantly to life. She stocks it with *Youki* soda, the only soft drink available. She flips the cassette in the small player to listen to more of Segovia while she practices reading aloud the New Testament in Moore, looking up words in one of the few hand-typed Moore dictionaries, testimonies to the tedious translation work of the early Protestants.

GENEBA'S DAY

The Fulani returns shortly after dawn the following morning, but Norago arrives early as well, his energy palpable. As arranged, Augustin already dressed in white, stops on his way to the clinic. The four of them introduce themselves and begin to speak about the condition of the baby, Thea entering in as best she can.

Communication has begun. The beautiful Fulani is Elisabet, and the infant is Geneba, a girl of fourteen months and weighing, Thea guesses, less than 2 kilos. After much talking and gesturing by Norogo, Elisabet agrees to Augustin's plan of care. Thea has prepared the milk, and for lack of anything else she has sterilized a Murine bottle to administer the drops. She brings it from the refrigerator and warms it in her hands.

Fully rising, the sun is hot. They find the shade they need under the zandi. Bravely, Elisabet loosens the dark hand-dyed cloth around the lethargic baby on her back and eases her to her chest. She hands her to Augustin who slips the baby to Thea, his hand cupping Thea's briefly in the transfer. They exchange glances in the midst of their shared tenderness for the mother and child. Something beyond their shared purpose passes between them.

Their faces hover over Geneba's ancient looking body. Her tiny chest rises and falls; the breaths are shallow, her stomach distended. Elisabet must hold the nose of the baby, "Like this," Augustin shows her. He pinches the nose and holds the chin. Thea squeezes the Murine eyedropper into the corner of Geneba's mouth but she doesn't swallow. A tiny rivulet of the thinned, sweetened milk dribbles out the corner of her mouth. They try again and Augustin flicks his finger against one little heel. The heel turns a deep blue, but the baby is startled and swallows.

They schedule a feeding every four hours. Thea explains through Norogo that she will awaken during the night to do the feedings. Elisabet agrees to return. Augustin points to the sun to indicate when Elisabet should come for the first feeding. Eager to play his role, Norogo describes the times for Elisabet and quickly fills in with a longer explanation.

At midnight, time for the fourth feeding, Thea lifts the mosquito net and places her feet on the grass mat covering the cement floor, slipping into a cotton shift she has had made at the market. She meets Elisabet beneath the zandi. The moonlight seeps through the grass roof like strands of gold. The silver in Elisabet's hair shimmers in the moonlight. Thea is tempted to touch its smoothness.

Geneba cries weakly when they feed her. Face to face, they know it to be a good sign. Elisabet nods. Without Norogo, they don't speak. When Thea returns to her bed, the silence invades, and she feels afraid for the responsibility she has taken on.

Thea has gained the trust of Elisabet, but not without notice. Elisabet comes, clapping at the back door with two young Fulani women with malnourished infants on their backs. They too show Thea their empty breasts. Faithful to his task, Norogo describes to them the treatment Geneba has received, and they immediately agree, handing over their calabashes, slipping their infants off their backs, ready to begin. The women speak quietly in short lilting sentences with each other. Beneath the zandi, Elisabet crouches beside Thea. They demonstrate how to begin the feedings; the women grow silent as they watch.

Thea needs extra hands. The next day, Norogo brings Rasmata, a young, pregnant Fulani woman married to a Mossi. Her hair is in the traditional five skeins, looped and pulled to one side. Her beads are bright, the same yellows and reds of her wrapped skirt. Her skin is bronze, and reflects the morning light. Unlike most Fulanis she has been to school and reads and writes.

After Norogo leaves for the day Rasmata comes late afternoons to spend her nights assisting with the feedings. Thea spends several nights with her until she feels sure of the process. They rarely speak, but working as a team, Rasmata intuits what is expected of her. The Fulani women wait sitting quietly beneath the zandi where the darkest shadows begin. Thea turns the key on the lantern to shine more brightly. She counts five mothers.

In her bed, from time to time during the following nights, Thea hears the low whispers of the mothers or the tiny cries of the babies, but she begins to rest more easily, relying on Rasmata.

Early one afternoon, standing together in the kitchen, Augustin tells Thea, "What you've accomplished by nursing Geneba back to health has resulted in Fulanis with their children coming to the clinic. Well done." He smiles.

Their glasses sweat in their hands, and Thea brushes the dampness onto her cheek. Changing his glass to the other hand, Augustin brushes her other cheek, spreading the moist coolness across her sweating forehead as well. He releases a strand of damp hair and smooths it back. In the stillness they can hear the shushing of Boukari's broom as he sweeps the yard.

"Do you mind that I come?" Augustin asks, still holding his fingers against her cheek.

"No," Thea manages, "I don't."

HEALING WATERS

In late April, soon after Thea's first good night's sleep, she wakens at dawn to shuffling feet, coughing and murmuring outside on her porch. Peering out, she sees a line of people, sickly and poor, from her porch to the zandi. Closing the louvers, she hurriedly goes about her normal routine wondering what is expected of her. She scrubs her face roughly, not yet fully awake. She brushes her straw-blonde hair into a knot. Coffee, she thinks, before anything else.

Norogo claps at her back door. She invites him in and hands him coffee with his usual dose of sweetened condensed milk. She spreads her hands at her side, asking him, "Why are they here? Who are all these people?"

"They want prayer, Mademoiselle."

Standing at the opened door, Thea sees that the people in line resemble those Augustin sees at the clinic except Fulanis are among them, contrary to custom. Mostly women and children, they stand silenced by the opening of the door. In a long white tunic, a blind Mossi man is being led by a small boy with a stick. They get in line, and the bare-foot boy stands immediately in front of his charge, planting his stick with both hands in front of him. A man with a gnarled crooked stick for a cane cranes his neck above the heads of others; a woman with a nearly naked toddler in tow bends and shifts the infant wrapped on her back; a man with closely-cropped gray hair shuffles forward in the short mincing steps of a Parkinson's patient. He purls the fingers of his right hand.

She carts a bucket of filtered drinking water from the house to the zandi. Every day Boukari pumps the water through a *Katydin* filter, and Thea boils it before she drinks it. She offers the purified water, and some in the back of the line drift toward the pail.

Thea stands alone in the doorway facing the mix of Fulanis and Mossis. Those Mossis who are not Muslim believe in Wennam, a God who oversees all; fertility spirits who govern the rain and the earth; and ancestors' spirits who affect the lives of their descendants. She thinks of the Christians from Kaya who have befriended her and wonders if they have discarded their old beliefs, whether they continue to sacrifice chickens, sheep and goats to the rain and earth, and if they continue the ceremonies to appeal to their ancestors. Is Jesus the only access to God, the Father? A first seed of doubt is planted, and she accepts it into the rich earth of her heart.

With trembling hands she begins. Some have what are probably malarial fevers and are warm to the touch. They need Chloroquine from the clinic. Several are congested, with harsh coughs, worsened by the dust. With Norogo at her elbow, Thea talks with each one, asking the name, discussing the symptoms. She questions a middle aged Mossi mother with thin sagging breasts about how long her child has been sick.

She prays for each one briefly in English, laying hands on their shoulders, using their names. She also prays for wisdom and guidance. To whom do the people think she is praying? She asks herself. She catches herself, pauses, and continues even though she knows intrinsically the mistakenness of her prayers.

A leper, missing fingers on both hands, reaches, touching her arm with a disfigured palm before Thea reaches him.

"Holy Father," she prays for a fevered child, perhaps two years old. "Touch this little one with your healing hand."

Turning to the mother who carries a child on her hip, Thea continues her prayer. "Give this young mother the wisdom to help restore her child to good health. In the God's name, I pray."

"If the fever doesn't go away, you must go to the clinic for medicine. If the baby develops diarrhea you must go as soon as you can." Norogo seems to take longer than necessary to translate, and the line moves slowly.

She continues personalizing each prayer and suggesting the clinic, knowing they are just as apt to go to a local healer as they are the clinic.

The blind man, Gesebyam, is last in line. His white tunic is clean and expertly patched; his hair neatly trimmed. He leans in to hear her better, his expectant face turned up into the sun. He takes his well-groomed hand off the shoulder of the little boy and reaches, exploring the air before him for her. The boy, who guides by leading with the stick, shyly backs up against the blind man's robe until it nearly hides him like a shroud. Thea takes the extended hand, soft except for the calloused tips of his fingers.

"What is your work?" She asks.

"I shell peanuts in the market," He says.

"Do you have river blindness?"

"Yes, river blindness."

At one time he was able to see, compounding his loss, Thea thinks.

"I'll pray that you have peace and that those who care for you are blessed including this child who leads you. Your blindness is incurable, but I see that you can see beyond what others see . . . especially when it pertains to the soul."

He withdraws his hand and searches for the pale, wooden stick, rubbed smooth on each end from use. Turning to go he smiles, deepening the etched wrinkles around his eyes, his face with its deep Mossi markings still turned toward the sun.

"*Baraka*," thank you, he says. "*Baraka Wennam*," thank God. He is the last to leave.

Turning to Norogo, she asks him to see if Augustin is available to come from the clinic.

Norogo returns, riding behind Augustin, hands free, legs extended. He swings a leg over the back of the Vespa, and is standing alongside Thea before Augustin turns off the engine. Dismounting, Augustin, already in his lab coat, checks his watch. Patients will be waiting by the time he returns to the clinic. But in his perfected patience he enters the back door, extending a strong, rather long handshake to Thea. He has already seen the line at her door, which formed before dawn.

Augustin turns to her saying quietly, "It's because of the babies, Thea, because of Geneba and the infants you helped. Word has spread. I can't advise you, but according to the elders in the market, some people believe if you touch them and pray they'll be *mage*, healed. I'm sorry, I couldn't have predicted this."

Thea has seen the elders, old Mossi men seated at the market every day. They represent the ancestors and mediators, their drums at the ready, three or four of them in white garb and small knitted caps on their grey heads. Stoically, they sit cross legged on mats in the same place all day, smoking their pipes, chewing kola nuts, exchanging greetings with all those who come by. They are surrounded by bicycles that they guard while the men and boys market. They gather and pass on news and gossip, which spreads rapidly from one dogo to the next, even to the encampment of Fulanis skirting the village.

Augustin goes to check with Boukari at the well and leaves. Unhappy with the quality of water even after adding a holding tank to allow the silt to settle before being drawn the second time he considers digging deeper and lining the wall with brick and mortar.

A DIFFERENT SCALE

Geneba begins to have a normal appetite. Thriving, she has even taken to sucking on two middle fingers. She can now suck one of the bottles Augustin has brought from Ouagadougou. Thea sterilizes it after each use and buys more milk. Geneba still feeds every four hours as do the others. Thea begins to feel the fatigue. Much of her time is taken up and she's done nothing toward making converts. Subconsciously the planted seed of doubt has sprouted, and it grows when she questions this peoples' right to eternal life, or justifies their right to worship God with Jesus as Mediator without being compelled to repent.

She wants to compare Geneba to other infants her age. So, at her suggestion she, Norogo, Elisabet and Geneba visit the clinic and wait in the sun in a long line of patients to see Augustin.

As he examines the baby, Augustin says to Thea, "Geneba is one of the first Fulani to visit the clinic in Kongoussi."

He runs his finger along Geneba's gums, saying, "I can feel the buds of the new teeth."

Norogo translates, and Elisabet smiles. Geneba, at 15 months, is growing jet black hair in place of the rusty-colored stiff hair, a telltale sign of Kwashiorkor. Thea reaches to touch the downy new growth, smoothing her hand over the Geneba's head. Her fine features like those of her mother are filling out, the edema in her cheeks decreasing.

Balanced on the scale, Geneba reaches with both hands for Augustin's dangling stethoscope. She weighs 3 kilos. She smiles and stretches toward her mother. Elisabet has woven red beads into her own hair. They tumble forward as she reaches for Geneba.

Having received Augustin's guidance, Thea and Rasmata fill out the paperwork and begin to enroll the mothers and babies in the clinic. These mothers, too, agree to go to the clinic and get progress reports from Augustin. Rasmata's presence begins to ease Thea's fear and her deep longing to belong. Still, she needs to relate what she's doing to her calling that she had believed was to win converts to Christianity.

When Augustin comes in the afternoon his face searches hers.

"I pray for each of them and I encouraged some to come to the clinic. Do you think they'll come?" She asks, handing him a drink of filtered water.

"Norogo told me you're encouraging them to come. I guess we're a team now..."

"But I'm not doing what I came here to do," She says. "I came to show people the way to God. I should begin to start a church .

The Kaya Christians have been so supportive. I can begin to do that under the zandi they've built. I didn't mean for people to believe I can heal by praying for them. My time is all taken up." She doesn't expect him to answer. The silence is strong but comfortable as they drink together.

"Eventually it will be important to build a wall," she says, breaking the quiet.

That evening Thea bathes with a bucket of tepid filtered water, lathering her breasts, her long, thin arms and legs.

"That one is pretty," She heard a young man say to his companion in the market place about her several days ago.

Her forearms are slightly red from the morning sun, but tanned in contrast to the rest of her body. Reflected in her only mirror, she is thinner. She has always been aware of her tallness. She leans in and touches her cheeks. The tiny wrinkles around her eyes are white streaks against her now bronzed face. She and Elisabet have an aquiline nose in common.

There's a gnawing in the back of her mind reminding her that she's not doing what she came to do. Sent by a single congregation of people who knew her as a child, she knows they expect her to establish a church, telling the story of a risen Savior, the story of Jesus, the son of an only God who sacrificed Himself for their sins. Instead she has become complicit in the myth that she can heal with a simple prayer, a myth that has spread through the village and the encampment of the Fulanis. She's deeply involved with the malnourished infants they bring her. The Mossi villagers call her the *Nasare Tipda*, the white healer.

Thea begins to build a wall in her mind about initiating the founding of a church. Conflicted and confused about her role in the daily prayer line, she smooths *Nivea* cream onto her arms and props her feet on a stool, still adjusting to the exposure of wearing sandals every day. She rubs the lubricant between her toes and spreads the cream onto her shins and up her thighs. With her fingers, tugging gently, she massages the remainder of the lotion on her hands into her blonde pubic hair, and it shines like corn silk. She applies *Joy* perfume, to her wrists and neck, wondering if Augustin notices and recognizes her favorite scent.

Briefly, she anticipates Augustin's next visit, thinking of his dark unmarked face, the strength in his arms and smooth warmth of his handshake. She chooses another of the cotton shifts and redirects her mind to the complex consequences of her presence here.

She has yet to hold a service, but she is affecting people every day in a way she can't define or defend. The people who come to her improve, and the rumor that she can heal by laying on of hands is bolstered. How will she tell those supporting her that she has attached herself to the clinic and the physical well-being of those she encounters rather than their souls?

The congregation believes she is ministering to the heathen but, in her defense, she thinks, she hasn't encountered the imagined heathens alluded to in her youth, 'hungry,' the traveling evangelists and missionaries often reiterated, 'hungry for the Gospel.'

In the morning, again her devotional time is interrupted by the prayer line. She kneels beside her bed in the heat of the day when most people are napping. "Grant me the wisdom to know Thy will. Show me the path forward." She reads the story about Thomas who doubted the risen Savior. Would that *she'd* be invited to thrust her hand into His wounded side. Her doubts about an only Savior are too strong to dismiss. How can she teach what she doubts?

Both the district and national Board of Missions have denied her request to be sponsored as a single woman and come to Africa alone. Her appeals were poorly received. Her home church in Cathlamet, Washington, a congregation of about two hundred, her father on the board, has decided to support her as a single person for a one year mission, a year now since her ordination. After much investigation, she had learned of the DuPrets, well-founded Swiss Protestant missionaries in Ouagadougou, Upper Volta. They had welcomed her correspondence, unlike the American Protestants, and after much discussion helped her choose Kongoussi, a small Mossi village in the bush, ten kilometers from the thriving church in the village of Kaya.

All those years that she sat in the pew, sang in the choir, taught Sunday school and throughout her studies at college and seminary, she had a clear vision. She envisioned founding a church in an African village for people who hadn't heard the story of Jesus. She imagined that their heathen hearts would be wide open; pagans would be readily converted. They were just waiting for the good news.

Once here she finds a people with a rich heritage, thriving families, and a people resilient, content with a belief system affirming their lives, even though suffering the deprivation of a drought over several years.

After praying again beside her bed, before retiring that evening Thea goes out into the night and sits under the zandi seeking the company of Rasmata. She has, in times past, waited on the Lord, waited for impetus as they did in the upper chamber at Pentecost. Fifty days they waited. Her praying and waiting seem irrelevant to her here. Her days become busy, and she abandons her daily habit after that evening.

Beneath the zandi, the Fulanis who have come with their infants sit in the darkest shadows waiting. Her eyes adjust to the near dark where Rasmata works. Notebook in hand, Rasmata takes the lantern from post to post, a moving halo beneath the haven of the zandi, tending one baby and the next. A quiet intimacy prevails between Rasmata and Thea as Thea simply watches, finding purpose in the scene before her, the nurturing of starving infants.

Geneba is absent, no longer in need of Rasmata's intervention, but Elisabet, radiant with hope, continues to come in the nights, helping as needed. Rasmata and she chat in Fulfulde, a language not related or close to Moore. She brings the milk and will take no payment for it.

THE WHOLE
OF THE SKY

Rasmata, now seven months pregnant with her first child, still bends over easily and leans down to swaddle an infant in preparation to feed him. She is the last of thirteen children. Her father has three wives and three families permanently settled separately in Kaya after exchanging his herds for land. Rasmata had an education in French because her older brother had retrieved her from the bush and had chosen for her to live with him in Ouagadougou where an education was available. There had been no public school in Kaya. If not for him, she might have been one of the women under the zandi, desperate to keep a child alive.

Thea has noticed that Rasmata is more animated whenever Abdul, her first love, swings by on his bicycle. He often comes and goes to check on her. Thea develops affection for him. By marrying, they've broken with all tradition. Their first child will be one of few: both Mossi and Fulani. Rasmata has given up many of her customs, but her dress is typically Fulani. She wears a Fulani woman's traditional silver in her hair along with her colorful beads.

Thea has bought a tarp for the zandi and she can smell the mustiness of the sweating straw beneath it as she sits with Rasmata in one of the two creaking wooden chairs. Interrupting the silence, Thea leans forward on her elbows and tells her of the prayer line and the mornings' events in French.

"This all happened in the course of a day," she recounts, "And Augustin tells me that I am being called the *white healer.*"

Rasmata listens as she uses one of the newly purchased eyedroppers to feed the bundled baby. His appetite has returned, and he roots toward Rasmata's ample chest, trying to suck the eyedropper. "This one is ready for the bottle," she chuckles.

"The village people and the Fulanis who came to me this morning should be going to the clinic, not coming to me. I know the traditional healers use herbs and elaborate prescriptions, including sacrifices. Not knowing what else to do, I simply pray."

"Bush people have nowhere to turn, and they're slow to have faith in the clinic."

As Augustin has told her a lot of their views are held over from colonial days when it seemed everything about their culture was being challenged. The clinic represents that transformation and time of confrontation. Local healers, they accept. Augustin's influence is widening but slowly.

"Sometimes I lance and dress a sore or blister, but most of them need to see Augustin at the clinic. I guess it's all the same to them, thinking that I am one of the local healers who provide care on par with the clinic. It must seem so mysterious to them how one immunization can prevent measles, or how medicine can heal an earache."

"C'est vrai," It's true, Rasmata responds. She, too, has heard the rumor about the laying on of hands by Thea, the *white healer* from America. "They want to believe you have power from

God. They don't realize we have taken specific steps to get these babies well.

You have an opportunity, Thea, like no one else, to demonstrate the difference, the importance of immunizations as you say, the necessity to at least filter the water through a cloth, how to treat a fever or diarrhea. So many infants die of dysentery and dehydration."

Thea leans back, crossing her arms, holding herself as if she is cold, as is her habit when making a decision, though the night air is warm. "Can you begin coming during the day?" She asks. "I'll find someone else to come in the night. With Augustin's help, we'll start registering each one who comes to be prayed for into the clinic. I think they'll accept being registered and being seen by Augustin. Many of their health issues are about cause and effect, which we can teach when they come to us. Treating the water is the most important thing."

Happy just to have a salary, Rasmata tells Thea she, too, wants to see some of the attitudes of the tribes change toward each other as well as the clinic where Augustin practices the white-man's medicine. Now she can resume her normal routine and be at home at night. "Oui," she says. "Mais oui."

Thea tries to sleep but the heat awakens her and her thoughts disquiet her. The air is still. She hears the steady drone of mosquitos outside her net. She throws off the thin quilt and walks barefoot around the house. She revisits the morning's events: her almost daily encounters with the blind man, Gesebyam who seems to come every day; the man with leprosy. She remembers the somber faces of the worried mothers, realizing she has made a significant change in direction by undertaking the task at hand. Her original goals to *win* them to the Lord have been put on hold.

She picks up Oswald Chamber's *My Utmost for His Highest*, trying to find ease for her stretched, confused soul. She can't focus. Putting the well-worn devotional back on the small crate she uses for a bedside table, she extinguishes the lamp.

In the darkness the night sounds seem closer, and she can hear the mixed tones and slow beat of someone squeezing and beating the "talking drum." She has extended her budget. She holds back developing a plan to start a church. She has hired Boukari, Norogo, and Rasmata. She needs a wall, like everyone else, especially if she wants to hold services. She, herself, has too little privacy. The zandi has become a gathering place.

By morning she is exhausted. She rises earlier than usual and tampers with the refrigerator. With it running, she can cook ahead and not worry about killing a guinea fowl every day. She can take care of the milk properly. She can cool the Youki soda she offers Augustin at the close of his day at the clinic.

She hears Boukari's bucket clanging against the well and is reminded of her full day. Boukari has filtered out the silt and is heating the water for washing clothes after she goes through the prayer line. She checks to see if she has enough *Omo* soap for two loads. Her head aches, and she takes *Tylenol* with her *Niviquine*, the daily malaria prophylactic.

Again she stands in the doorway, facing the prayer line. The same after same people come daily. Having learned to treat guinea worm, she releases the dressing from Hado's atrophied leg and carefully turns the stick holding the exiting guinea worm, preventing it from retracting. Norogo hands her a fresh dressing, sent by the Women's Missionary Council of her home church.

She has learned from Augustin that some weeks later, as she continues to wrap it, the worm will be fully removed but Hado will limp painfully for several more months. At her side, the irrepressible Norogo chats on, as he is given to do, and reminds Hado not to go in the lake and to filter the drinking water with a cloth. Hado nods. Thea is unconvinced that many take her advice about filtering water. "Even for cooking…" she repeats.

She turns to the closed face of a crippled boy, Issac, one leg shorter than the other. His outgrown crutch has rubbed his armpit, and the sore is infected. Thea cleans the wound, advising him to go to the clinic for an antibiotic.

She meets the jaundiced eyes of a victim of hepatitis. He must see the Doctor at the clinic she says and eat no fat. "Your liver must heal and it will take a long time," advice she thinks he won't need, so weakened he seems.

The Mossi farmers have begun to plant the weary soil. The seeds are fewer this year because as the drought wore on they had to eat some of the stored seed they would have planted. But the rains have begun to break the long drought's hold. Coincidentally with the Mossis' planting, as the grass returns, the Fulanis, family by family gradually pick up their domed *barrukas* and return to their way of life in the sub-Sahara, grazing their herds over an undulating landscape, from one watering hole to the next according to ancient patterns. Mothers with babies who are not thriving stay behind forming a small community of their own.

She picks up a letter from La Poste. Seeing it is from her father, she rips it open and reads it standing in the stale air of the post office.

Dear Thea,

*I hope this finds you well from your bout
with malaria. Your mother and I are fine.
The yearling calves are fattening and it
looks as if the beef prices will hold.*

*I know it is unusual to hear from me rather than
from your mother. I just came from a board meeting.
There is concern that you are overly involved in
the physical needs of the people, which can never*

*be fully met, in lieu of actually presenting the
gospel. I wanted to tell you firsthand so that you
are not only prepared for a letter from the board
but also, I'm hoping you will become emboldened
and more willing to put yourself on the line.*

*You must feel so alone in this, but our prayers
go up daily for you. You can do it.*

Love,

Your dad.

She turns the thin page over. It is so unusual to hear from
her father. In fact, he has never written to her here in Africa.
She sees he has used his fountain pen and is suddenly, nearly
overwhelmingly homesick for them. She takes heart from the
loving tone of his letter, but doubts her first purpose in coming
here the more.

Soaking up the more frequent, gentle rains, the savannah
beyond the cultivated fields turns a creamy green. Rasmata
and Thea have only a short time to affect the Fulanis' attitudes.
Elisabet and Geneba come one last time to say goodbye, and
Geneba leans to reach for Thea with both arms. A joy fills her.

In need of someone for the night feedings, Norogo presents
Araba, a petite sixteen year old Mossi girl, a Wednesday's child,
who has gone through the sixth grade. Araba speaks Fulfulde.
Her breasts firm, the dark nipples curved upward, she walks
as if she is stretching to be taller. Her buttock is rounded and
high, like a shelf, causing her wraparound skirt to hike up in
the back. She retains the plumpness of adolescence in her round
face. Rasmata will train her for a week before she changes her
own schedule.

After the prayer line the next day, Thea notices two Hausa
traders from Nigeria lingering outside the zandi, their packs on

their backs. They're thin and sharp featured, scantily clad. After she prays for the last person, they spread out their goods on the zekka: beads of many colors and sizes; cowrie shells; bracelets of ivory and brass; silver coins, deeply black ebony carved antelopes; wide toothed wooden combs; a variety of statues and masks.

For its beauty, Thea bargains for a figure of wood and brass, a nearly naked well-endowed woman with a high headdress. She thinks that perhaps these pieces of art originate from the playing shadows around the evening fire. After walking away from the Hausas several times in the bargaining process, she agrees to pay half their first price. She also purchases an ebony letter opener for her mother.

The figure, a Karan-Wemba, is carved for the burial ceremony honoring an elderly woman, meant to appeal to her ancestors. On a base it stands alone. Thea places it in the small, sparely furnished living room in the middle of the bookshelf at eye level. She watches out the louvers as the traders repack their merchandise and follow the path to the market.

Thea and Rasmata work hand in glove and spend long hours together, succeeding as they have in staving off the starvation of these few Fulani babies. They work also to enroll the very sick into the clinic so they only have to stand one line to see Augustin. Rasmata works seven days a week, tending the babies as if they were her own. Thea, too, is comforted, like the infants, by her strong presence. Thea's prayer life has diminished to an afterthought, and her doubts about having been called of God to minister the Gospel have increased. Perhaps the message is less about redemption and more about connection.

"Come and meet Abdul's family," Rasmata invites Thea. "It's a short distance from the market."

"I will if you teach me to dance," she laughs.

When she arrives at their walled cluster of round dogos, Rasmata's mother-in-law and sister-in-law are pounding grain for *sagabo*. Rhythmically, with long wooden pestles, they throw them in the air, clapping before the pestles hit the mortar, singing as they crush the millet. They stop when they see Thea at the entrance. Thea walks across the flat, red-clay yard as they welcome her, and call for Rasmata.

After they proceed through the greetings, Thea is offered a turn to pound the millet. They laugh together at her clumsiness, but she eventually succeeds at throwing the pestle in the air, clapping as it comes down. They don't suggest the complications of singing along or adding anyone else, so that Thea might learn to throw and pound in time with the others without hitting their pestles.

Having finished their task with the millet, Rasmata leads and dances to an unfamiliar rhythm, music made with tambourines and sticks by the others. After being invited Thea joins them, and they demonstrate more complicated steps, speeding up the rhythm.

Thea is shown each woman's dogo. Rasmata's is filled with wonderful fabrics, some folded, some tossed on her pallet, and some hang crookedly on the walls.

Thea excuses herself as the sun sets, before they build up the fire and begin their meal. Looking about her once more, Thea compares the structure of her parents' home: the high ceilings, the picture windows, the step-down living room, all her father's design. She recalls her own room, its neatness and familiarity.

Later that week, Thea and Rasmata are invited by a group of young Fulanis to go out among the cattle when the moon turns full to celebrate the cosmos. For the occasion, Rasmata fits Thea with a yellow, black, red and white wrapped skirt. She braids tightly some of the strands of hair around Thea's face, weaving in beads the colors of her skirt. Standing back, she claps with approval. "My sister," she says.

They walk together with about fifteen Fulani youths onto the plain where the cattle are kept. A deep yellow, the moon hangs huge and low on the horizon. The cattle come bawling and mewing when called, forming a circle around the group as they are seated on the new grass. The cattle nose in and nudge their backs. Their breath, warmer than the night air, is pungent and moist. The sweet, fresh grass blends with the musty smell of the cattle.

Each of the herd has a name and Thea is introduced: Ranne, the white cow; Baale for the black one; Taureau, the fast one; Oole, the straw colored; Woune, the slowest. The steer is called Oudjiri and the head of the cows is called Kalhaldi.

As they sit cross-legged, the varied colorful woven cloth worn by both the young men and young women spreads out around them, muted by the moonlight. Thea is transported by the flute music. Such a gentle people, she thinks. They pass a drink in a gourd and the smell is yeasty, like rising bread dough. She sips, passing it to Rasmata, on her right.

Kalhaldi seems most interested in the flute player and stops chewing his cud, lifting his dark head when the music begins. The profile of the boy playing the flute who is nearly a man is lit from behind by the rising moon; it is a fine profile, evoking pride and strength. His shoulders lean toward his own music and his beautiful head yields to its high and low notes. He seems to be bowing. Dipping his body, his pursed lips take short breaths, and he holds the flute he has carved, closely against them, sighing into the reed's mouthpiece. His slender fingers slip up and down.

Rasmata reaches for her hand, covering it, holding it close to the earth. The moonlight leaches Rasmata's face, and it is radiant. Thea takes her eyes off the flute player and looks to the sky, conceiving, and yet not, the magnificence of the universe. Fixed in the heavens, the stars are opal and the sky a vast cloth of velvet. Is that a sprinkling of gold dust in the far reaches? Her soul has paused as if to see beyond herself without an encumbering body, free to be amazed and to delight in being alive. But more, she is in awe of a presence much like she felt when she felt her calling. Neither defined nor denied, there is a presence. The group lingers, quietly lingers.

How long has the light taken to get here? Raane, the white cow, nudges her shoulder, like a living ghost in the night.

THE CURIOUS AND
THE BEGUILED

From the kitchen door the following afternoon she sees Augustin walking toward her, favoring his leg more than usual. Two young boys tug at his pants, wanting to see his stethoscope. He kneels and each listens to the other's heart. They jabber together over the magic of it and scamper away off the path, into the shallow ditch, still slippery from the last rain.

He enters the kitchen, and she quickly begins telling him of her experience under the stars in full moonlight. "Augustin, I've never. . ."

"Slow down, slow down," he says, taking her by one hand. The kitchen is narrow. He turns and opens the refrigerator with the other, pouring the Youki into two chilled glasses. She's behind him and bumps him as he turns to hand her a glass.

Finally, she sits on what has become her side of the table, the back of her hands flat against it. "It was transformative, Augustin, like no other experience I've ever had." She waves her glass after her first swallow. "I feel smaller as a human but enlarged as a spiritual being. I can't explain it."

I've always thought of our world as being the center of God's attention. The concept of the universe has never really played a role in my faith or how I try to acquaint myself with Him."

"More than humbling, isn't it, being on the Sahel on a moonlit night? He says. "When I was a boy, I was lost once and found my way home by the stars. I think I prayed there, exposed like that, more intensely than I've ever prayed, not just for my safety but in awe."

"Oh, Augustin, then you know what happened to me. I prayed too, but to an all-consuming being, a different prayer than I've ever prayed. It was truly transformative. There are billions of stars and planets, I know that, but I was struck by the reality of such vastness. Infinity. . . I knew suddenly that I will never achieve understanding or knowing God. I felt humbled, but wishful too, that my life could be significant in some way, amidst the grandness of it all."

When she pauses for a breath, Augustin leans across to her. "You've altered my world forever, Thea. I can't tell you how hopeless I felt until you came. It's as if there's an invisible charged thread between us. You have encouraged me in my work to bring health care to Kongoussi. But more than just me, I've seen you touch others. You've altered my way of seeing things.

I see now that touching someone in a loving compassionate way is the very touch of God. I'm actually encouraged as a bush Doctor that what I do has meaning. Your touch and, I hope, mine, are healing, and the body is more likely to heal when spiritual healing takes place. I've seen a lot of people who want to love God without ever achieving love for other people. You've touched *my* spirit and I find myself seeing my patients through your eyes in a whole new way."

Augustin walks into the open space of the sparely furnished living room, picks up the carved art Thea purchased and speaks back to her in the kitchen, "Not only do you own a sacred statue, the Karan-Wemba, you've been to a Fulani worship service," He teases. In the doorway he cradles the Karen-Wemba. "Are you certain you're not a pagan yourself?"

Thea has unknowingly purchased a sacred statue, thinking of it only as art, not associated with the spirits of the dead. She feels spooked. As a born-again Christian she has drunk from the fermented potion in the beautifully etched calabash they had passed around, but hadn't thought she was participating in a ritual, worshipping some other God or gods. She hadn't understood the significance of what she had done.

Confounded, wishing she saw more clearly the portent of her decisions, she turns her back to him. She yanks at the stubborn metal handle on the only tray of ice she has succeeded in making that day, the cracking sound matching her frustration. They carry their sweating glasses of orange soda to the zandi.

"The congregation wants a report on what I was sent to do," she says. I must begin holding services under the zandi. Almost everyone I know has written and asked about the founding of the church."

He has seen the stack of thin blue aerograms from her home church, from her parents.

"My letters to them seem nearly false. I've been so caught up in the everyday lives of people; I'm not fulfilling my mission. Augustin, I've told them of these hard times and how much suffering I see each day. I've described the new season beginning and the hope that is rippling through the village. I've talked about the beauty of the language, but there are no converts to report. I've yet to tell anyone the story I came to tell."

"Maybe the story you came to tell is changing. You don't see your effect on others or the contribution you're making because you're too focused on the idea of building a church.

Maybe God is working with you and through you and you don't know it."

Strong-minded that she is, Thea believes that nurturing the infants and conducting the prayer line have been deterrents, and that the success of her mission will be a growing group of new Christians, a church in the far reaches of Africa, like her dream. In one frame of mind, she abandons the idea of one Savior. In another, she struggles with the obligation to hold to her first vision and the expectations of her home church.

"I'd like to begin to build the wall. I've saved enough to begin. Otherwise we'll call too much attention to ourselves. I won't know who really wants to hear and participate from those who are curious."

"It all begins with being curious, doesn't it?" He responds.

She pauses briefly, "I think beginning the church is going to happen sooner than I thought. Pastor Barri of Kaya has sent word about Sidabé, a young Mossi minister, trained by the Protestants in Switzerland, willing to come weekly and preach. If he's successful he'll move his family here."

Come Sunday, Sidabé will come," she tells him. I'll play my accordion, which will attract a crowd for sure. Sidabé and I'll sing from the French hymnbook, which just might turn them away," she jokes.

Augustin seems amused. Slightly smiling, but gently he asks, "Why build the wall? Isn't that what you wanted, the whole village to worship your God?"

Thea can't respond. She knows that she has been derailed and that her faith in Christ, as Savior and herself have eroded. Her calling seemed so real at home. Now it seems misplaced and naïve. She retreats to her deep affection for him.

"Tomorrow," She asks. "Will I see you tomorrow?"

"Oui, demain. "

Augustin has decided to have the men begin digging the well more deeply and confers with Boukari before he goes. She watches him, his arms crossed, feet wide apart. Until they hit rock, the water won't be clear. She believes in Augustin's determination to make it happen.

She changes the ribbon and labors over the dusty typewriter writing a letter to her friend, Sheila, not knowing her own heart. Smudging the paper from the ink on her hands she whips it out of the typewriter and balls it up. To her parents she talks much about how Rasmata has become like a sister, someone she'd like to bring to the states someday. She speaks of hard-to-know Araba, her commitment to the night feedings and the efficiency of ever-present Norogo.

To the missionary council she writes:

Dear friends,

*I have written before of those who come to me
with their medical problems, wanting me to
pray for them. I can't tell you how much your
support of me has meant. Because the package
was large I had to pay some duty for the strips
of dressing you sent, but I use them every day.
I will be able to use more in the future.*

*The light-weight quilts are working out beautifully.
There's just enough difference in the temperature
day and night to need something, especially toward
morning. I have given the yellow and blue one to
my friend Rasmata, who has worked so hard.*

*Once the sun comes out, watch out! It is hot. I have
a tin roof so my little home becomes like a cooker.
I am lucky to have the zandi I told you about.
I often sit under it late afternoons, and we use it
still for the mothers who come with their infants.*

*The rains themselves have changed, from pounding
hard rains when the water seemed to just run off,
to much lighter rains. The whole savannah looks
different, certainly more habitable. As I told you
the Fulanis will slowly return to migrating. In the
meantime, a dozen or more mothers have remained
behind. The Mossis are planting the millet. It is very
rich in protein, unlike corn. Excuse me for rambling.*

*The small caps you knit for the babies have
worked out wonderfully. We use them at
night, and we wash them and reuse them.*

*My own health has been good. I've had touches
of malaria with a low fever and headaches like
none other I've ever experienced. After a couple
of days I am good to go. There's nothing quite
like having a fever when the weather is already
sweltering. It's important to drink lots of water.*

*Filtering and purifying the water is a hassle but
many of the chronic diseases are carried by the
water, so it is extremely important to be careful
with what I drink. We have only one carbonated
beverage. It's called Youki but I call it yucky, it's
so tiresome. Knowing I don't drink the water, the
villagers serve me Youki if I am a guest, and, of
course, it's warm. They pour more and keep the
glass filled after I've had a couple of swallows. It
is expensive for them so I take a few sips and
stop. Sometimes, even though it's warm I want to
glug it down, but they just refill it to the brim.*

*I realize I'm running on but I want to say a
big thank you to all of you. I recognize Ragna's*

*hand in many things, so a special thank you
to her. I would love to receive your letters.*

In Christian love,

Thea Lancaster

★★★

On a Sunday morning in June, her first attempt at a service and
shortly before the expected arrival of Sidabé, Thea prepares the
zandi. For the pulpit, Boukari upends a rain barrel and places it
in the rear. She situates the two wooden chairs just behind it.
Atop the barrel she places her largest cutting board. She places
one of her Mother's handkerchiefs over that but it blows away.

Sidabé comes on his bicycle. He stands behind the makeshift
pulpit momentarily, opening his New Testament with its goatskin cover on the cutting board. Finally, they go through the
formalities. Thea sees in him an earnest, well-meaning, young
man. Barely acquainted, they begin.

The wheezing accordion on Thea's lap seems to intensify the
heat as she begins playing, her lips mouthing the words, "I love
to tell the story of Jesus and his love; I love to tell the story of
unseen things above . . . To tell the old, old story of Jesus and
His love."

Sidabé, at the front of the zandi, ushers in those who are
coming, Fulanis among them, instructing everyone to sit in
straight lines. Surprisingly, the Mossis greet the Fulanis as well
as each other and make room. Sidabé leads the nursing mothers
to the back. Thea hums as she plays "On the Old Rugged Cross,
the emblem of suffering and shame. . ." and wonders why the
straight rows, why the nursing mothers in the back? Sidabé is
imitating what he saw in Switzerland no doubt.

Sidabé stands behind the barrel pulpit wearing a grey, limp suit. His narrow crooked tie is red. The wool suit hangs longer than his arms. The perspiration has begun to seep though at the arm pits. He mops his face with a nearly white handkerchief. He is younger than Thea had imagined him to be. She wishes---and thinks that he wishes too---that he were wearing wide-legged pants and a fugu, like most Mossis.

Intense, Norogo translates from French to Moore to Fulfulde, taking longer than seems necessary. Thea reads a passage from Saint John from the Moore New Testament. The goatskin has worn to a sheen. "For God so loved the world". . . Norogo translates into Fulfulde.

Sidabé chooses to preach about Zacchaeus. He opens the New Testament, using the authority of a book, and shows them the page, "When Jesus, the Son of God, walked on this earth, he had many followers, people like you who wanted to hear and know more."

Norogo walks the width of the zandi with Sidabé, back and forth, waiting for the pauses, his cue to translate. Going from the French to the Moore to the Fulfulde takes time. Thinking of a solution, Sidabé asks for those who speak Moore to raise their hands. Everyone there except for the Fulanis raises a hand.

"I'll preach in Moore and faithful Norogo will translate to Fulfulde," Sidabé says to those huddled in under the zandi.

After this interruption, he continues. "Jesus was in Jericho. The crowds had gathered around him, each seeking his attention. A rich tax collector, who was very curious about Jesus, felt a tug in his heart to see Him for himself. He had a hard time seeing because he was short so he ran ahead of the crowd. When that didn't work he climbed a sycamore tree. Today, many of you have come because you're curious about Jesus. Jesus sees you and is calling out to you by name, just as he called Zacchaeus by name."

Holding up the worn New Testament once more, he continues, "Lo and behold, Jesus saw Zacchaeus in the tree and called to him to come down. Jesus invited Himself into Zacchaeus' home, which was unheard of. Zacchaeus was a public tax collector, a known sinner. People thought Jesus would be impure if He went home with Zacchaeus. The crowd murmured and complained. But Jesus went, and later, as they ate together, Zacchaeus repented of his sins. He was sorry for overtaxing people and keeping some for himself. He had grown rich by imposing too many taxes on the poor.

But Jesus forgave him. It was by the grace of God that Zacchaeus was called down by Jesus. It is by the grace of God that *you* are here today. *You are being called.* Can you feel the tug in your heart that Zacchaeus felt? Jesus is asking to come into your heart. Your sins will be forgiven as you repent to Him, and He will dwell within you."

He asks those who want to invite Him in and receive Christ as their personal Savior to stand. Even the nursing mothers stand.

While they stand, Sidabé realizes the metaphor about inviting Jesus in hasn't quite conveyed what he wants to say. He tries to clarify his message, stressing the part about repentance. He asks those who don't want to repent to be seated. Somewhat confused, Norogo interprets, and adds an explanation of the importance of their decision. Confession and submission are required. They will be expected to give up their old beliefs, he says in Fulfulde. Sidabé is surprised and puzzled about Norogo seeming to add his own thoughts, but he nods in agreement.

Many resettle cross-legged onto the zekka. Sidabé prays for the souls of those, mainly young men, who remain standing. He invites everyone to return the following Sunday. The group of onlookers straggles away after the sermon.

When Thea sets aside the accordion the more curious come to examine it. Thea demonstrates how the buttons and the dusty, yellowed bellows work on the old purple instrument. Some drink from the water with the ladle before they go, wiping their chins, shaking the water from their hands.

Augustin comes late the evening after the first service. They sit in semi-darkness under the zandi. Thea says, "Their rituals have so much meaning. How can I, with an up-ended barrel begin to up-end their beliefs? If Christ is not the only way to God, why should we?"

"For the most part they're open-minded, and welcome what you have to say."

"So it's traditional to welcome me? If that's the case, I won't know where they're coming from. They responded well to Sidabé. It was crowded under the zandi."

"Maybe it's more about belonging than believing," Augustin responds.

Inside herself, she acknowledges her own need to belong here among the people of the village.

Thea wants Augustin to stay longer and offers him a cup of Sanka. But he goes.

FOR THE
COMMON GOOD

Some weeks later as Thea finishes her lesson in Moore, Augustin
is talking with Boukari. Thea brings the three of them a Youki
soda. Boukari holds the chilled bottle against his cheek, his
usually sober face changing to a grin.

"I couldn't ever live here without Boukari's help. I hope he
knows that. *Ne toumde*, Boukari," good work.

When they leave Boukari, they talk again of the services. "I
think it's a good sign that Sidabé has exchanged his wool suit
for something more comfortable. Now they're making their
own music spontaneously. I'm only playing my accordion at the
beginning. I can't compete with the drums anyway, especially
the talking drum," She laughs.

"Augustin, they have such a spirit of belonging. I'm puzzled
by their cohesiveness. I don't think I'm outside the circle, but
I'm not the driving force. There's a dynamic I hadn't anticipated. I'm afraid I know too little about the culture to ever
understand, let alone be given credit for the existence of this

group of believers. It kind of founded itself. Thank God for Sidabé because I can't believe in the same way I did.

They're mainly young people. Maybe with the rejection of the old ways, there is a need to replace them, as you said, to belong to something larger than them. What do you and others think, really, when I don't know all the details of the customs you follow? Even so, they treat me as if I'm a saint."

"Thea, if you tell them your father didn't teach you something, they'll understand your inability to know their ways. They expect the same from you. For instance," he chuckles, "you wear short dresses." He clears his throat and smiles. "That's considered provocative among the Mossis but the exposed breasts of the village women aren't. While you wouldn't show your breasts, they wouldn't show their legs. No one expects you to change your habits, although it might be interesting." He rubs his chin as he does when he's pleased with what he's said. She feels charmed and defeated in the same moment.

"Interesting?" she says clasping her hands around one knee, aware that her bare legs are crossed.

"You are rather attractive, you know, in spite of your pale skin." He says.

Thea clears her throat. "Going back to the services . . . Shouldn't we begin with a gentle shepherd instead of teaching Jesus is the only way to salvation?" Thea asks. She wants to present God differently than how she was taught to believe. Contrary to the message she came to bring, she wants people to understand that God is just as available to those who haven't heard the gospel as to those who have.

She wants to deviate from her former belief that the only way to Him is through repentance and the acceptance of Him as a Savior. She determines to translate the 23rd Psalm out of the Old Testament. She wants to present her image of God as a shepherd who cares and guides everyone. But still, a shepherd is only one image.

Like the prayer line Thea faces every day, she feels she has lost control of her situation. "I just don't believe what I've been taught all these years, that they will perish unless they accept Christ as their Savior."

"I think your doubts will lead you forward not backward," Augustin says. The sun resettles itself into the feathery pastel bed of night, and Augustin moves to go.

NORTH AND WEST

Thea is finishing a particularly long prayer line when Pastor Barri, the pastor from neighboring Kaya, enters the yard, riding a dusty well-used bicycle. The tires are worn and the kickstand is missing, no fenders. Thin and agile, the pastor is well groomed, his white smock intricately hand embroidered, although he is covered with a thin layer of red dirt. His face is open and warm, the tribal marks deeply etched into his cheeks, the skin inside the scars darker than his already dark face. Appearing to be about sixty, his hair is partly gray as if it has been sprinkled with ash. His shoulders are hunched as if he is still on the bicycle. Laying the bike down, he proceeds through the greetings.

Glancing toward the last of the line, he offers, "Let me help you finish."

He prays with a strong, raised voice, placing the heel of his hand on their foreheads. Sometimes their necks jerk backward and they seem dazed. After he finishes, feeling loyal to them, Thea talks with each of them quietly, remembering their names and their problems.

Finished, they sit beneath the zandi. The chairs have scuffed the zekka, and she toys with the crumbles of clay with the tip of her sandal. Boukari will tend to it tomorrow. Certain Pastor Barri has a purpose for riding the ten kilometers, she waits until he's ready to disclose it.

"We need to thank you for the zandi. We use it every day, and the church has started to meet here. Thank you, too, for sending Sidabé. I think he should move his family here. He seems like the right person to help the church get started."

He says, "The ones who come have told us they want to build a brick church here."

"I didn't realize they were ready." She remarks.

"If they want Sidabé to be their pastor, the Kaya Christians would be willing to help make bricks and build the walls. You probably already know that Augustin has donated the property across from you. The big expense will be a tin roof. Thatch won't work because the rains will ruin the bricks if they're left uncovered."

Thea is surprised. Neither Augustin nor Sidabé has discussed with her the possibility of actually building a church. Trying to contain her feelings of shock, she says "We only want God's will." Do they sense she is no longer committed to the gospel proclaiming a single Savior?

A church would demonstrate the success of her mission to others though she can't take credit in her own mind or soul. She hadn't known that Augustin was communicating with Sidabé and the converts about the possibility of property. Given its location so near the main road and the market, the property is valuable. In spite of her, the church is becoming a reality. Flummoxed, she says, "But that's not why you came. You have another reason, don't you?"

Finally, after still more conversation about the prospects of a new church here in Kongoussi, Pastor Barri settles his mind and reveals his purpose in coming.

He brings an invitation from Pere Blanc, the white priest in the northern village of Ouaihagouya.

Cheres Mademoiselles:

We are pleased to invite you to come to Ouaihagouya where an influx of Fulanis has temporarily gathered around the mission compound waiting for the distribution of food. The mission station will be a distribution point for cornmeal contributed by the US through the Catholic Relief Services (CRS).

Many of the infants have symptoms of Kwashiorkor and their mothers will be waiting about the compound. Hearing of your success, we would appreciate your counsel regarding the infants."

Pastor Barri is obviously pleased he has been asked to deliver the letter. He smiles broadly while she reads the letter.

"The Pere Blanc would like you to come the day before the next distribution when the women begin to gather. The food will be distributed in the measure of a calabash per person every three days."

This point of distribution at the mission has been carefully chosen by the CRS, and the word has spread. They have also heard the rumors of Thea and Rasmata's work and success with the infants.

"I'll check with Rasmata right away. There's no question we'll go. Please stay for dinner and sleep in the compound. Don't bike home at night. You can leave tomorrow when we do."

"*Baraka Wennam.* Thank God. As God wills," he says. "*Ya laafi bella.*" It's good.

Abdul helps Thea and Rasmata find a car and a driver at the central lorry stop. That afternoon Augustin makes his weekly trip to Ouagadougou and agrees to bring back fresh vegetables and ice.

Later, Thea prepares a meal of rice and chicken for Pastor Barri, and they sit in the kitchen conversing as best they can without Norogo until they see the bouncing headlights of the Peugeot returning from Ouagadougou. "You are truly God's gift to us," he says to Thea, standing to retire for the night. Seeing Augustin's trunk full, he helps carry the abundance into the small kitchen. Thea sorts while they talk. She'd like Pastor Barri to leave but Augustin leaves first.

The morning they leave, they pack the vegetables for the mission station in the large, green Coleman cooler and pack their food and filtered water in a smaller one. Rasmata brings rice with a meat sauce, and Thea prepares the small filet of beef Augustin has brought. They take bread and an especial round of imported Camembert from the Bon Marche in Ouagadougou and protective clothing for mosquitos, in case they get stranded. Lastly, they pack eyedroppers and drooling cloths, small, hemmed squares of cotton fabric sent by her friend Ragna Rodahl and others of the Women's Missionary Council in Cathlamet.

The driver, Jacques, whom Thea judges to be about thirty years of age, arrives after dawn, wearing a watch and Polaroid sunglasses. He carries a battery operated tape player and a pocket of tapes. He is without tribal markings and wears a dress shirt and pants with a belt. His shoes are worn but polished, his car, an old, black Mercedes, probably bought in Ghana and imported years ago. He speaks French, but not as well as if he'd been to a formal school.

At dawn, as the people wanting to be prayed for gather, Norogo, at hand, is proud to say that Thea and Rasmata will be on a trip to Ouaihagouya to help more babies. They break away from the line, murmuring in assent as the word passes among them. "*Wennam taas laafi*," God give you a safe journey, they say to Thea one by one.Norogo moves quickly to offer water as Thea would do.

Abdul accompanies Rasmata into the yard to see them off. He admires the car, and Jacques opens the gleaming black hood to show Abdul the nearly glowing clean motor winking back at the sun. Children have gathered, mostly little boys, and they take turns looking at themselves in the side mirrors, laughing and going back to the end of the line again and again.

"*Ya soma quai,*" It's really nice, Abdul exclaims as they pull down the hood. Abdul shoos the children away and uses the corner of his smock to wipe the fingerprints off the side mirrors.

Abdul and Norogo load the trunk, placing things alongside an extra five-gallon tank of diesel. Inadvertently, Thea has left out the Camembert cheese. She puts it in her straw bag and slips into the worn, black leather seat in the back, relieved to see the air conditioner. Rasmata settles in beside her.

As they are pulling out, Augustin arrives, dismounts and leans into the car looking for Thea. "God give you a safe return," he says patting the side of the car.

But before they pull completely out, Thea notices the ever humble Pastor Barri standing by the zandi. "Do we have room for him?" Jacques stops, pulls ropes from the trunk, and ties the bicycle onto the car. Thea is relieved. She had forgotten her offer

Pastor Barri says, "This is God's blessing to me. I have the Lord's work to do in Kaya. Thank you, Thank you." Once on the road, Pastor and Jacque's conversation is indistinguishable for the roar of the diesel engine, but Thea hears talk of Jesus in the front seat. If Jacques isn't a believer now, he will be before they arrive, Thea thinks.

When they reach Pastor Barri's compound in Kaya, he spontaneously leans over and says a prayer over Jacques before he gets out of the car. Rasmata and Thea exchange a disbelieving glance. Has the very modern Jacques been converted in such a short time?

Jacques helps with the bicycle. Reentering the car, he says, "I thought we'd never get here. I've had my sermon for the day. In fact, I think I just converted to Christianity."

After leaving Pastor Barri in Kaya, Rasmata and Thea try quoting the 23rd Psalm and laugh when they stumble. "Speaking of shepherds," Thea asks, laughing, "What *is* the difference between a sheep and a goat, anyway?

They both look the same, thin and scraggly as they wander about, sniffing the air. They don't appear to be shepherded at all. Maybe the good shepherd won't resonate with the new Christians after all."

"It's easy: the goats' tails go up and the sheep tails go down," Rasmata demonstrates with her hand, "Otherwise, they look the same."

As Rasmata and Thea talk, the subject of the Sunday services comes up. Rasmata, a regular attendee, suggests, "Let's encourage Sidabé about allowing people to sit as they'd like when they come to service, rather than having them in rows. And let's encourage him to let the impromptu indigenous music flow even more."

Thea is relieved that someone holds her same views. She'll be glad to put aside the accordion. They can create their own services well enough already.

"I'll be glad to hear some drums and tambourines. But I can already guarantee you I won't be able to sing along."

"Teach me to play the accordion," Rasmata says, "After the baby."

Rasmata talks of Abdul's way of catching her unaware and slapping her buttocks.

"He's always catching me when I least expect it."

"I can't imagine Augustin doing that," Thea says but wishes she could.

Rasmata catches her arm, looks her in the face, from one eye to the next, and says, "Tell me the truth; I think he cares for you and you for him."

Thea directs their attention to the Camembert, meant to be a gift for Pere Blanc, which has begun to soften and run. "Oh, dear," she laughs. "We're going to have to eat this. Jacques, can you stop? We need a baguette from the back. It will take all three of us!"

The cheese is too soft to eat gracefully, and before long they have it on their fingers and running down their chins. They have put a cloth over the hood and lean over it. They finish one of the Pere Blanc's baguettes. "The Pere Blanc doesn't know what he's missing," Rasmata jokes.

They have traveled two more hours when they begin to see women walking north toward the mission station, one by one, no longer on a footpath but alongside the road, dressed in dark, hand-dyed, indigo blue with empty calabashes swinging at their sides. Jacques slows the car each time they pass to decrease the wake of dust. By now further into the Sahel, it swirls in clouds the color of dry mustard.

In another hour, more are walking single file. Surely, the word is out about the coming day's distribution. Jacques slows to 40 kilometers per hour, lengthening their trip. They feel the bumpiness of the washboard road at the slower speed and the dust invades the car. Rasmata and Thea grow quiet watching the thin dark figures walking such a distance.

Arriving, the car is surrounded by women wearing nothing but the near-black Indigo blue, short, wrapped skirts. They stretch out their arms and spread their hands open to say they have nothing. They lift their empty breasts. In tears, Thea says, "Rasmata, you go first."

Thea doesn't open her door. Rasmata cracks hers open and plants her feet on the ground. She speaks with one of the women and the others back away with the lethargy of the very hungry, allowing Thea and Rasmata to pass into the yard of the compound. The women somberly return to join the others seated in a large, silent, ragged circle. The absence of sound is only attended by the small cries of their babies.

Jacques opens the trunk and lugs the large cooler behind Rasmata and Thea as they approach the compound.

"Bien venue," the Pere Blanc welcomes them. He is a slim man of about fifty, a sharp face and a long chin disguised by an earthy red beard. He is dressed in long, white garb, wringing his hands. Two young blacks dressed in shorter brown frocks and leather sandals step into the sunlight to greet them.

"How were the roads? Did you have rain?" The taller one asks.

"We were delayed by the number of women and children walking alongside the road," Rasmata says.

"The trucks certainly don't slow down for them. The people arrive here hungry, dusty and thirsty," the Pere Blanc says.

Adjusting to the heat outside the coolness of the car, Thea feels faint, quietly taking in the unimagined scene, noticing the prevailing torpor.

"Merci for the invitation to come," Rasmata says. They are offered water, but Thea prefers her own. Jacques is led away to other quarters with one of the servants.

In the foyer, Rasmata is happy to open the cooler and present the gifts. The Pere Blanc stands back with his arms folded while the two brothers squat over the insulated chest, their wooden crosses dangling, pulling out the lettuce, finding the strawberries. Their own gardens have suffered from the drought, and they haven't seen such vegetables in a long while. Rasmata shows them the long, orange carrots, their tops still on. She has brought a basket of ripening mangoes.

Rasmata and Thea follow through the corridor of the unpainted cement block home of the brothers into a large, high ceilinged storeroom, where as they expected, the dirt floor is covered with one-hundred pound bags of corn, imprinted with the *United States of America* SURPLUS, ready to be rationed.

The corn is not a good long term substitute for the protein rich millet or the milk products in the normal diet of the inhabitants of the northern Sub-Sahel, but it will sustain them until better times.

"By tomorrow," the shorter of the two brothers says, "We estimate, over three hundred people will line up to receive a portion. They've sat about the compound for two days, waiting."

"More will come," says the Pere Blanc.

Some of the smallest infants sag on the backs of the dehydrated mothers who can no longer nurse them sufficiently.

"Where are the loaves and the fishes? Where is the manna? Are these the children of Ishmael? "Thea asks angrily under her breath.

She turns to the brethren, "How many can you feed . . ." She pauses surprised that there are stacks of American labeled powdered milk along the walls. Outside are people starving, and inside is this large amount of rich protein.

She stops mid-sentence, angrily asking, "Why isn't this milk being distributed? Why can't this be used even right now today for the mothers and babies?"

Rasmata takes Thea's arm. She says, "Powdered milk will give the babies diarrhea, and they'll die of dehydration before they receive any nutrition. There's also the problem of keeping bottles sterilized when bottles have never been used." Rasmata embraces her lightly when she finishes.

The Pere Blanc nods in agreement with Rasmata. "We've tried and failed."

Thea's anger subsides. She acknowledges inwardly the sacrifice of these men called by their church to be here in what feels like a God-forsaken place. These men have no expectation of miracles. They have a grim reality to face daily, crimes against humanity that have no perpetrator.

"You must get so frustrated," she says, apologetically. The dining room is bare and close. The table they are shown to is crude and seems to have been built without the purpose of dining on it. Thea shifts her knees after she sits and angles them to one side of the table leg.

Their delayed, simple lunch, pate and baguette, is unaccompanied by any of the fresh food they brought. Gherkins sit atop the pate. Rasmata sits on the edge of her chair, not in the habit of eating with cutlery. She tastes the mustard condiment and Thea sees she doesn't like it. The cornichon bites back, and Thea pours water from her own flask.

Back in Kongoussi, Augustin will soon be through at the clinic. He had encouraged them on their mission-- Thea in particular-- but warned, "You'll be seeing hungry people who can't be helped."

As intended, the conversation at the lunch table centers on the dilemma of the many outside for whom there are few solutions. Thea explains the method Augustin has prescribed, plunging hopefully ahead. "To accomplish the same here it would take several young women willing to be trained, willing to spend the nights attending to infants. We feed every four hours. You have to introduce small amounts at a time so that the babies will adjust to taking nourishment."

"If you have a place for me to stay, I'll prepare the formula and teach the girls. We brought some supplies." Rasmata says.

Thea says, "Rasmata that would be so great. We could see if Jacques could come back to get you when you think you're ready."

Turning to the Pere Blanc, she asks, "May the women and babies who come for regular feedings stay the night beneath your covered courtyard?"

"That is such a kind offer," the Pere Blanc says to Rasmata. He turns to Thea, "Of course we have a place. We can certainly find some young women among the Mossis, *n'est ce que pas?*" Can't we? He looks to the Brothers.

Rasmata is shown where she'll stay, an unpainted room with a wooden slat for a bed. Against the bare cement hangs a mahogany colored wooden crucifix. The carved head of Jesus is tilted to the side; His feet are tied together; His wounds gape.

Thea helps bring in her things bundled in a cloth and lugs the basket of supplies. She lays a quilt on the cot, squares of blue and yellow. Ragna, her elderly Norwegian friend, in Cathlamet would be amazed at how far her handiwork has traveled.

Rasmata is still hungry and removes her food and water from the cooler and places it on the only piece of furniture, a small wood desk. The high window is metal louvered and she opens it. They embrace before Thea goes. "Send word by lorry when you're ready to come. We'll find a way for you."

Jacques and Thea drive into sheets of torrential rain. With only one windshield wiper, Thea can't see what's in front of them. They try to cross a barrage-- part of the road designed for the run-off during such a storm-- but the car spins and slides and won't go up the short incline. Jacques continues to try, gunning the motor, but the wheels slip and the car skews. The rain stops, but the run-off continues, and the barrage begins to fill. She suggests that Jacques push while she tries to steer out of the muddy slope.

Thea slides over and puts the car in low gear and rocks it with the clutch, and Jacque pushes until it grabs and slowly climbs the slope. He's removed his shoes and rolled up his pants, and his white shirt is splattered. He grins.

"Good work," he commends her.

Thea thinks back to the years she worked with her father when they had to get one of the farm vehicles unstuck. At least something of what she has learned is useful. With Jacques' mud-caked foot heavy on the accelerator, they are on their way.

Rocks and mud hit the car, but they leave no trail of dust for the drenched pedestrians.

They arrive later than expected. Augustin waits under the zandi, and appears momentarily in their headlights as they drive in, hands on his hips. Thea opens the car door before they have stopped.

"Welcome home," He says. With an arm around her shoulder, they walk toward Jacques who is worse for the wear, examining his prized car, unlike the dapper fellow he looked to be in the morning. "Well done," Augustin says to Jacques.

Looking at the muddy car, Thea tips him. "Bonne nuit, Jacques and thank you very much."

Jacque examines the money in his hand and grins.

Turning to Augustin, she says, "Rasmata has stayed in Ouaihagouya to build a team there to help with the Kwashiorkor victims. I need to let Abdul know."

Together, Augustin and Thea go by Vespa to tell Abdul the news. Having come from the cool car to the warmth of his back, Thea pulls in closer, the warm night air in her face.

"Rasmata will do well," Abdul says proudly, offering them local beer. "Those people are like family to her. She'll feel at home."

Augustin remains on the Vespa after they have returned to her dark house, still closed up. She lights a lantern. "Let's open the house up and sit under the zandi for a bit while it airs," she suggests.

"Let's," He says and she opens the fridge for something cool.

Outside the staleness of the house, they sip the Youki, and the nighttime air is balmy as if it has rained.

SALUT!

Rasmata sends word some days later, and Abdul arranges for Jacques to return to Ouaihagouya in order that she can come home more comfortably than by lorry. Abdul is becoming anxious about her pregnancy.

Because Augustin makes a weekly trip to Ouagadougou after his hours at the clinic, he can easily pick up more of the fresh vegetables at the grand market. Abdul makes plans to go along with Jacques.

The afternoon Augustin and Thea expect them to return they wait in the kitchen talking, listening for the sound of the diesel motor. Night falls, and they finally hear Jacques honking the horn as they approach her yard.

Rasmata and Thea embrace, then stepping back, each holding the other's shoulders, they are face to face, smiling. Thea pays Jacques, tipping him as before.

Abdul and Rasmata, arm in arm, crowd into the kitchen. Thea brings oranges from Ouagadougou out of the refrigerator and presents them stacked together in both hands. The fragrance is in the air and on their hands as they peel the thick skin away, pull back the spongy membranes and eat the segments, cold on their tongues. Thea feels the pleasurable slight tightening of her jaw in the first bite.

Spontaneously they salute each other, oranges in the air, touching one orange against the other all around. Rasmata has succeeded. The report is good. Exhausted but exhilarated she leans closely into Abdul. "The babies adjusted so well to the formula, and I've trained a group from a club of fifteen-year old girls to continue the work. An older woman, Fatima, is over-seeing them," She reports." Abdul encircles her and she backs against him, tipping her head back.

"Rasmata, its God grace, as Pastor Barri would say, that we have you," Thea commends her as a peer. Thea doesn't recognize yet that her own heart is invested here, nor does she notice the absence of the often curbed longing for home. Augustin feeds her the last segment of his orange, and she touches his hand as he reaches for her mouth.

It's early June, a Monday. Under the zandi, Rasmata perspires heavily as she finishes registering the last patient. The morning heat is intense and the patients have crowded her. The acrid smells linger as they begin to leave. She winces and places the palm of her hand under her swollen belly while encouraging the statuesque Fulani mother in front of her to take her feverish toddler to the clinic.

Rasmata is one of the first converts who Thea believes has made a commitment to Christ. During their work together, Thea shares the story of her calling as a child, her reasons for coming. Unable to be dishonest, she also conveys her doubts about asserting that Jesus is the only way to God. Rasmata likes the idea of a final sacrifice, becoming secure in her faith. As Rasmata accepts the idea, Thea quietly discounts its narrowness.

Neither Muslim nor animist, Rasmata understands the concept of a Savior, the very son of God who made provision for eternal life. As she helps Thea translate the Twenty-third

Psalm, she also comes to comprehend the notion of the Good Shepherd, someone taking tedious care of the sheep, not unlike the Fulani cattle loved individually and protected day and night. Thea is somewhat reassured by Rasmata's response and is drawn back momentarily to the soothing cocoon of her fundamental beliefs and the traditions of *her* father, which brought her here. She envies Rasmata's faith but is unable to reclaim her own in such a defined way.

Late afternoon, Thea and Rasmata walk the distance to the clinic following the one lane path that winds its way to the market and beyond to the clinic. In front of them, laughing and talking, are two Mossi women coming toward them, returning from the market, one with a pyramid of tomatoes in her head pan, followed by another with a typical round, multi-colored basket. The first in line turns her head back, trips on the root of an acacia tree, and the tomatoes spill, rolling across the beaten-smooth path and into the scrub. The two women stand back slapping their thighs, laughing. Rasmata laughs with them while curving her back, her hands supporting her hips. Thea helps pick up and restack the large ripe tomatoes wishing she shared their immediate camaraderie.

Thea and Rasmata talk easily as they walk single file to the clinic. Turning her head back as she holds her hand under her belly, Rasmata questions Thea about the Old Testament, not yet translated. "There are so many stories you'll love," Thea tells her, "Especially about the Israelites led by Moses who wandered in the wilderness, much like your people in the present who migrate and have no place called home."

"Their home is the desert and the whole of the sky," she responds.

Of late, Thea has noticed Rasmata wincing with the typical Braxton Hicks contractions, small and infrequent, that often signal the baby will come soon. The baby has also dropped.

"The baby's lower than a week ago," Thea remarks. "Is every-thing in place for the delivery?"

Rasmata replies, "Everything is good. I'm having small con-tractions that Abdul's mother tells me are normal. Abdul holds my belly at night to feel the baby move. He believes we'll have a boy. He can hardly sleep, so I tell him to go back to his own dogo," She chuckles.

"I'll be attended by Mossi midwives. Three days after the birth, according to Mossi custom, we'll name and present the baby."

Thea wishes she would be examined by Augustin. She wonders too if Rasmata would rather have Fulani midwives, but she'll have no say. She gives up her traditions for Abdul's. Rasmata appears secure and contented. Although he could have others, Abdul pledges that she will be his only wife. Thea observes their easy banter and their bond.

TUESDAY'S CHILD

Augustin is sterilizing the syringes, ending his day. The clinic is immaculate, newly whitewashed. In a corner an aged Mossi woman stacks fresh linens and after gathers the day's soiled laundry into her basket and swings it on top her head in one fluid motion.

Surprised to see them, Augustin grins broadly. "Welcome," he says. Unbuttoning his lab coat, he calls for the laundry woman to wait and throws it up into her basket. "*Baraka*," he says to her, thanks. "*Wennam kota beogo*," God give you tomorrow.

Their evening baguette in hand, Abdul, looking for Rasmata, comes wheeling in on his newly acquired, bright red moped. "Ne pongo," Augustin congratulates him, as Mossis typically do when someone gets something new, touching the shiny front fender with the tips of his fingers. Deliberately, Rasmata climbs on behind Abdul.

As they part, the two say, "God give you tomorrow," almost in unison.

Augustin turns to Thea. "And you? Are you *laafi bella*?"

"*Faan ya laafi*," everything is good.

"The Fulanis are coming to the clinic and the Mossis are accommodating them. When they return to migrating, they'll know they can come back here in a time of crises." He remembers to take off his stethoscope and hangs it near his stool.

"May I give you a ride home?" he jokes, smiling. "Mine is not as shiny as Abdul's but it will go faster. I notice Abdul and Rasmata are doing well, thanks to her salary."

"Rasmata is due any day. "Thea says, already anticipating seeing less of Rasmata. "A baby is forever. Nothing will ever be the same for them. It becomes your world, a child . . ."

Augustin responds, "Let's hope for an easy birth. If she's born tomorrow, she'll be nicknamed Tuesday's child."

"I was born on a Tuesday." Thea responds.

"Then we'll call *you* Talato," Augustin grins, holding her chin.

Thea pulls her shift as high as she needs to climb on the bike. Augustin reaches back to her and asks if she's ready. They tour the small lake and start to circle back home. Thea grips his waist and bends with him on the long curves.

Because of the mosquitoes they don't stop even though the lush, hand-watered gardens are inviting. Malaria carrying mosquitoes abound especially around the murky water. "The abundance of mosquitos precludes sleep, and according to legend the village was named as it was because Kongoussi translates literally to 'cannot sleep,'" Augustin leans back and tells her. He touches her thigh lightly with his left hand as he rounds a turn.

Part of the receded bank is muddy and trampled by the Fulani cattle, and a few of them stand knee deep, guarded by a boy with a stick across his shoulders.

Augustin stops near the cattle, and the Blackcaps perched on their splotchy colored backs fly away. The boy waves without taking his hand off his stick. The silence between Thea and Augustin seems fixed since he reached back to touch her leg.

His strong presence remains a mystery to her, and she finds his silence quieting. Still she breaks it. "Do you pray?" She asks stepping off, looking at him directly. Some of the cows begin to amble toward them tossing their heads, flicking off the flies with their tails.

"Only to an unknown," he answers. With the back of his hand, he touches the muzzle of the black, red and white spotted heifer, obviously ready to calve. He runs his hands along its belly and the flesh twitches. The flies leave again and resettle. "Nearly ready," he says to the animal and pats the animal lightly on its shoulder. He raises a hand to the boy standing nearby and says in Moore, "Good Luck," even though the boy won't understand.

Neardusk, when they return, Norogo waits in the zandi. "Rasmata is having the baby. The baby is coming."

Thea turns to Augustin saying, "Won't you stay until we get further word? I'll make a small supper. Norogo, you as well."

"Let me get the car in case Rasmata needs to go to the hospital in Ouagadougou," Augustin replies.

While he goes, Thea makes sandwiches from a baguette, her hand-whipped mayonnaise, left-over guinea fowl and tomatoes with a light swipe of Dijon. Norogo, in a hurry, pedals off, biting off the end of his sandwich as he goes.

"I'll be back as soon as I hear," He calls.

Thea heats water for coffee, a light odor of kerosene in the air before she strikes the match. She feels the anticipation of being with Augustin.

When Augustin returns, they eat at their familiar places at her kitchen table. "Tell me more of your story," she says, pushing away her coffee. Looking him in the face she asks, "How did she die, Ophelia, your wife?"

Scraping his chair back, he begins, "Three years ago, this month, we were walking home from the market in Ouagadougou and we were hit by a Frenchman driving a Landrover. We were both taken to the hospital. She died on the way. I had my leg broken. She was buried the next day by our families here in Kongoussi in one of my fields. I was six weeks in the hospital.

"I had been working at the hospital at the time. When I recuperated it seemed best to come back to my home village and family. My two sons teach in the new school here and their families are here. With the insurance payment, I built the clinic." Augustin turns his head to the wall.

"I'm sorry, I can't imagine your loss, and those long days in the hospital must have been nearly intolerable," Thea says, swallowing hard.

Augustin covers her hand. "We can only pray for tomorrow. Here and now I am sitting with a beautiful, woman, whom I adore."

Thea rises, saying huskily, "But *you* built the clinic? I thought it was government owned."

"Now, the government has acquired it, after a long struggle to get their support."

"And your boys started the school…?" Thea asks

"We lived in Ouagadougou when they were young. Although it's now in shambles, they were able to get their degrees in Education at the university. Through our families and our properties we had many ties here in Kongoussi, and they set their hearts on beginning a school here." Augustin says.

She broaches the subject of the property he will donate. "Why," She asks, "When you're not even a believer?" What is the genesis of his generosity and goodness?

"People will get weary and stop being interested if there's no room under the zandi," He answers.

Thea pursues her question. She understands his generosity, building the clinic, staffing it without pay until the government became involved. She also understands that he could practice medicine in Ouagadougou or outside the country and make a good deal more money.

"Augustin, that's hardly an answer."

"I've seen this kind of church change a village. Everyone benefits. Children can learn to read---Did you know that if you learn to read in one language that it's much easier to learn a second language? Have you seen how the villagers are supporting each other, even sharing seed to plant? The church under the zandi is good for all of us."

"I think there's an underlying reason, something more---" Thea says.

"I am a believer, but not in the way you might think. My grandfather, Pierre, was not a Pastor, but he helped found the Protestant church in Upper Volta in 1914. He was a little like Peter, don't you think, to whom Christ said: 'Upon this rock I will build my church'? Because of him and the missionaries, one in every three Mossis is now a protestant. They have built schools all over the country."

My father, Jeanne Paul, was well educated as you might expect, and began investing in cotton and gold. He bought a good deal of land here in Kongoussi but leased out all the crop-bearing fields. After his success as a business man, he studied in Switzerland and became a protestant minister in Ouagadougou in the church his father built. By then he was 45.

As you see, I've inherited a good deal I didn't earn."

His voice falters as he speaks. "Like you, I was raised as a believer in Christ, but after Ophelia died so suddenly, I came to understand that God can seem absent. You say the premise of your calling is that all are lost without accepting your gospel.

I believe finding a way to God is what's important, not how, and that humility is what saves us from our mortal selves. This is not a repudiation of your faith, rather an affirmation that God means to be accessible.

Until He was more than an abstract notion, none of the purported ways to worship or pray meant anything to me. Hopefully, the people who come under the zandi are actually seeking and will find God each in his own way, whether they mix their belief systems or not. How can it matter which faith we choose, if the outcome is people caring for one another here and now, and that certain peace that come with believing.

I became a Muslim when I married Ophelia. Her father insisted. After she was gone, I faced a new reality. I'm doing this now because my own faith is renewed, not in Christianity but in people who have compassion, like you. You don't know how you have encouraged the residents of Kongoussi. I expect you never will."

"The ratio of boys to girls in school is about three to one. The girls often drop out at puberty and unless we can build some private toilets, they won't be back." Augustin says.

"Pierre is the school master. Jean Paul is most qualified to be the math teacher, but he teaches first graders to read as well. Sometimes the brightest ones are able to be guided in a self-learning curriculum and they advance quickly."

"Do the government officials recognize the need for latrines or is it all about boys?"

"Often the parents can only afford the boys."

"Pierre and John Paul go off on some weekends to help dig a well or build a latrine for a school. Getting the village chief's support, which hasn't been easy, is important."

"Speaking of changes, you've changed a lot of people here in Kongoussi. Whether I believe or not, your little church has become quite a place."

"I don't feel that *I* started the church. I think it started in spite of me. "

Thea thinks about Rasmata wondering if her labor has progressed.

Augustin and Thea talk over several hours and it is late, nearly midnight, when Norogo claps loudly at the back door, then bangs against the metal.

"It's not going well," he bursts. "The baby is stuck."

"BLUNT NOT THE HEART"
WILLIAM SHAKESPEARE

Augustin swoops up his keys, Thea turns off the lantern, and Augustin takes her hand to go. Norogo leads the car on his bike, his headlight feeble and wavering, legs pumping hard as he stands on the pedals. The powerful beams of the Peugeot reveal a large snake curled alongside the road. Thea shudders. Leaving the road, they bump down a path between the closely-set dogos. Augustin parks as closely as possible to Rasmata's dogo.

Thea follows Augustin as he carries his bag along the unlit footpath that runs along a shallow ditch. A scruffy dog barks and tags along. They reach one of the midwives standing at the door of Rasmata's hut; she is talking with the women attending Rasmata, hands gesturing. Rasmata's labor has progressed but she cannot dilate. Her cry is guttural. She is on her elbows, pushing.

A wave of nausea surges in Thea's stomach and she feels faint. The hut is small and hot. She smells the sweat, the blood, the feces. She goes to Rasmata's mat and kneels down, touching her forehead. If ever she wanted a prayer answered, it is now.

Rasmata's skin is grey and without its usual luster. Perspiration coats her forehead. Her hands are cold, and her forearm is cool and damp. Rasmata collapses back onto the mat, without strength for the next contraction. Dark pools of blood have puddled on the zekka. Her stomach heaves as a contraction rolls through her.

When she was five years old, Rasmata had been circumcised according to an age-old uncontested Fulani tradition. The clitoris and labia minora have been removed. The outer lips have been stitched together to cover the urethral and vaginal entrances. A new opening has been created for the passage of urine and menstrual blood. As a consequence she is obstructed, a condition known in modern times to be linked to the scar tissue of her circumcision.

The Mossi midwives have not seen this type of circumcision. By Mossi tradition only the clitoris is removed, and the surgery is done at birth. They talk excitedly among themselves.

Augustin sees they have been called too late and shakes his head. He places his fingers on Rasmata's wrist, holding it for a long moment. Lesser contractions continue, but she sinks into unconsciousness. Her breathing changes, punctuated with stops and starts. They watch helplessly as the stertorous breathing stops altogether. With a deep sigh she passes. They wait in poorly lit silence, and another breath does not come.

Abdul is drinking the local beer with his friends when Norogo finds him.

"Abdul, come quickly. Rasmata needs you." He cries.

Augustin meets Abdul, steering through the crooked path between the houses on his red motor bike. Augustin, facing him, his broad hands on Abdul's handlebars, says, "Rasmata has died. The baby is gone. Time ran out and I had no time or way to save her or the baby." Augustin steadies the Moped as Abdul leaps off.

Abdul tears at his shirt, ripping it down the front. He tears at his hair and kicks the bike. He cries in anguish.

The midwives have begun to mourn in song. One leads with a verse in a minor key, and the others come in later singing the same sorrowful phrase; each verse is a new composition, accompanied by Abdul's weeping. He sits on the ledge of her doorway, his arms wrapped around his head.

Rousing, Abdul seeks out his family, and they begin the burial process, which will by custom take place the next day. They will dig the grave through the night in one of Abdul's inherited fields.

Thea has stayed near the body, not yet releasing Rasmata's lifeless hand. She turns to see Augustin standing, shoulders slightly slumped, waiting. Her heart wrenches toward him, toward his exposed soul, that of a man who knows personal loss, one who feels the sting anew. She pulls one of the favored, printed, colorful cloths strewn about to cover Rasmata's face.

Thea reaches the car before Augustin. It, too, is stifling as she waits for him to console each member of the gathering family. She makes a keening, mewing sound, then a larger noise, like the wail of a child with a hurting heart. She holds her face with both hands. Her beautiful Rasmata. Gone. A victim of an uncontested rite meant to give her marriageable status as a young woman.

Augustin finally comes and turns the motor. The fan blows loudly. He turns to face her, taking one arm away from her face. She pulls it back and faces the window to her side. He follows the bumpy path until they are on the main road. The air conditioner has begun to work, and he turns a vent, directing more of the cool air toward her.

Pulling alongside the road, he stops the car. Their dust catches up with them and briefly clouds the headlamps in the light breeze like a spirit leaving the earth. The car running, he reaches for her with both arms.

"Talato," he says.

His face is as wet as hers, and she smooths his tears aside as her own tears run unchecked.

They hold each other, and then he is caressing her. She cries in confusion, her loss comingled with her desire for him. He releases her seat to recline and leans down toward her. She responds, pressing her wet face against his shirt into the pit of his arm. Reclining his seat, they lie together in silence, their vision blurred, grieving, one, comforting the other. His hand strokes her hip, and she can feel his hardness against her thigh. Sitting up, trembling, she turns the vent of cool air directly into her face.

Norogo pedals up to Augustin's door. Augustin cranks open the window. The warm night air blows in. "Is everything alright?" he asks. His young face is wet and contorted in sorrow.

Pulling out his handkerchief, Augustin wipes his face, nodding. "Everything is fine." The usually light-hearted Norogo rides away uncharacteristically slow, and Thea sees him draw his arm across his face, wiping it with his sleeve. He, too, loved Rasmata. They pass him slowly to reduce their dust. Augustin has left the window down, and she can hear the crunch of their tires and the gravel chink against the underside of the car.

"The funeral will be in the open sun." he warns, as he leaves her to face the night. "*Wennam koto besongo*," God be your help. Thea feels physically weak as well as afraid of the night.

The trill of wailing, the ululating of the women announcing the deaths of Rasmata and her baby is a sound like no other, perhaps like wolves, penetrating the night, reverberating in Thea's chest. The throbbing drums keep double time with her heartbeat. Rasmata is being mourned in the village, and Thea is alone in her bed.

Thea's faith has failed her, and her grief is corroded by anger. She longs for restored faith in the Gospel, the clarity she has lost. But there is no way back. No longer able to simply trust her heart, she thinks of the audacity she must seem to have, how ludicrous, coming here to challenge long-held customs and rituals of worship with a newer better way, a gospel proclaiming to be the *only* way to eternal life.

Could some small change in the chain of events have caused it to not end so tragically? Would it have played out differently had she not been here? Surely, it would have. Trying to dig more deeply, she feels powerless and betrayed by God who is supposedly all powerful, yet personal enough to "call" her to the ministry.

She doesn't hear anger in the village voices decrying death, only desolation. But she is angry. She writes in her diary a quote from Shakespeare's Malcolm to Macduff: *Let grief convert to anger; blunt not the heart, enrage it.*

Continuing, she writes her own verse:

> And in the void was anger,
> Not God's but mine.
> He righted the chaos of darkness for Himself
> By simple declaration:
> Let there be light.
> After all, why not?
> I would have righted my own chaos,
> Should I had found THE words,
> Should I have had THE power?
> Like Solomon,
> While I slept,
> Someone has shorn my hair.

She thinks of Augustin, his dark, chiseled face above her own in the car. Grieving, she is more vulnerable to feelings for him, and she is stretched to a new sense of selfhood. She draws up one of Ragna's light quilts, and turns on her stomach, wanting to cancel her need for him. She twists the quilt into her fist. Loss and love combine in her dreams, as in life.

MANGOS IN THE AIR

Augustin and Thea attend the burial together under the ruthless sun in an open field, the newly planted millet swaying in a light breeze. A Djeli sings. The drums, the stringed instruments and the wooden xylophone accompany, and the masks, round faced, vertical planks of red, white and black, dance and weave among them, in attendance to honor Rasmata, giving her admission into the world of ancestors.

According to tradition Rasmata is not in a coffin. She is wrapped in white cloth stretched tightly over her head and body, over her pregnancy. Rasmata, a new Christian, is buried according to Mossi tradition.

A distraught Abdul does not want to leave her body. The grave has been dug deeply enough for a shelf to be made inside, protecting the joined bodies from being ravaged by hyenas. The bodies are placed on the shelf, and the men cover the grave with red earth. Abdul turns his back and doesn't participate. He shrugs off a hand on his shoulder.

The funeral concludes. Thea and Augustin shake hands with each member of the family as they file by. "*Wennam koto be songo*," God help your heart, they repeat the traditional consolation. Abdul is not with them. Thea notices the heaps of gifts for the family placed at Rasmata's dogo.

That afternoon, Augustin returns and remains seated on the Vespa with the motor running, hesitant until Thea invites him in. Closing the door, they embrace, a long embrace; she raises her face to his, knowing him now in a transformative way. The smell of *Vetiver*, the cologne he wears, and the now musky odor of him stir a deep, familiar wanting. She turns to open the refrigerator, resorting to their routine.

Standing behind her, his hands on her shoulders, he turns her, takes her chin and kisses her deeply, gently drawing her tongue inside his mouth. She can feel the tug on the root of her tongue. He gathers up her shift, and with a hand against her buttocks, pulls the length of her toward him. "Talato, my Talato" he says. He kisses her neck and leaves abruptly.

Beneath the untreatable hurt of Rasmata's death is an underlying hope. He obviously cares for her. No matter the outcome, she thinks, in the morning she will stand at the doorway before she prays for those who wait to be healed, not knowing to what avail. The repercussions of her love on any ministry she might have are unfathomable. Or perhaps her real calling is different than her imagined one. Maybe it *is* life-long. Maybe God's will doesn't need to be defined and characterized by her. Maybe it's as simple as following her heart. Her heart tumbles after Augustin.

Already and through the course of days in June, Rasmata is missed for her gentle, sure ways, for her robust energy, her glowing beauty. A nerve is touched when Thea sees a pregnant woman on the path. Adrift as if in fog, a small canoe in a churning sea of doubt, she grieves for Rasmata. She is buffeted as well by the sheer need for Augustin's steadying presence, the price of it incalculable.

Her feelings of love for Augustin continue to influence her every thought. As she works with Araba, or as she studies the language, she is conscious of everything about herself. How would Augustin see her? She stands over the sink, peeling back a mango, letting its thick, pulpy juices run onto her hand, pressing its soft, giving flesh against her lips, and she thinks of him joining her in such a simple pleasure. She uses the mirror more frequently, turning to the side, touching the pink nipples, lifting a breast as if offering it to be suckled. He continues to come. The tension rests between them whether they talk or they are silent.

In late June, it is even more obvious to Thea that the health of most of those who come to her each morning is improved except for a handful, mostly younger men, who come with a disease known as "slim." These patients don't improve, and as they sink into anorexia, their mouths develop sores that don't heal. Rumors are that there are many more patients with the same syndrome in the city. Cancers grow on their skin, deep brown uneven patches. Augustin and she speak of its mystery, and Augustin is frustrated about how to treat them, watching them decline, not knowing how to help them or if they are infectious. These patients eventually lose hope and stop going to the clinic with their fevers but they return to the line until they die, sometimes in the zandi. Boukari is quick to return their bodies to their families. He heats water and scalds the zekka where they have lain.

Araba works hard but not intuitively alongside her during the nights until she is trained. She calls Thea as she is known around the village, the *Nasara Pinda*.

"Call me Thea," Thea reminds her, but she persists. As the Fulanis return to migration, there are fewer and fewer infants. Soon she'll not be needed.

Norogo seems to notice Araba and hangs about past the time he is needed. Thea finds them with their heads together at dusk, sharing a sweet under the zandi. They break apart but their hands are touching.

"My two employees seem to be falling in love," Thea tells Augustine. Augustine whacks two ripe mangos from the neighbor's tree. He drops his stick, and they drop into his hands.

"Hmmm, I wonder how that feels," throwing the mangoes like a juggler.

"Maybe it's in the air." She presses the satiny softness of the mango he hands her and puts it to her nose.

"I wonder who caught it from whom?" He asks.

"You had it first," she lies, walking behind him single file.

"You may be right, He laughs. He has not kissed her since the day of Rasmata's funeral. Surely, he, too, is as conflicted as she. How would she be received by his sons and their families? Now the silences that fall between them seem uncomfortable and unfillable.

"Back to Norogo, he's been a great help at the clinic when he gets time. I've taught him to take vital signs. He would be a good employee, good at detail. I could teach him to draw blood and take specimens, freeing me up to get more done. I wish he could train formally, but I'm afraid he wouldn't do well in Ouagadougou without family.

Ouagadougou is becoming a hub for restless young men who are leaving their old way of life in the village in hope of something better. Shanty towns are springing up. They've no chance of being educated or finding work. I'm afraid we're seeing a new generation who are rejecting the traditions but aren't grounded in anything else. There isn't much of a future for them either in the fields or in the city. Here in Kongoussi your church is making a difference. The young men joining seem to have real purpose. They want to build schools. They want better medicine for the village. They're inspired, and making lasting friendships."

Thea can't think of the church, detached as she is from the gospel Sidabé preaches.

"Hire Norogo if you'd like. It's a rare opportunity for him. I'm doing well enough in Moore that I can manage."

When approached, Norogo accepts the offer. Thea misses his ambitious presence, his quickness.

"You look like a professional in your lab coat," she tells him when he comes one morning after he has worked a week in the clinic. He comes for his sweetened coffee; but perhaps he comes to see Araba as she leaves after a night under the zandi. Thea takes her a cup as well. She takes it with both hands, smiling as she takes her first sip.

The next day Araba walks the path in front of Thea as they carry a collection of filled out forms for Norogo at the clinic to sort and file. Araba is quiet and seems to carry her bottom even higher. She swings it sassily from side to side.

When they arrive at the clinic Augustin is tending to the cut in the arm of a small boy. He finishes sewing, snips the thread and dresses the wound. Thea watches his smooth hands, wanting them touching her, wanting him to respond to her body again.

Araba, by now has been engaged in conversation by Norogo. They don't seem to notice Augustin locking the clinic. They'll have some time together before Araba spends the night under the zandi, Thea thinks, happy for Norogo. They walk off together, Norogo pushing his bike. Araba's headdress is especially high today.

Augustin says, "If you'll wait a minute, I'll drive you home on the Vespa."

Thea accepts the offer. When they arrive at her back door Augustin does not dismount.

"How about a Youki before you go?"

He hesitates and says, "In a minute. I need to talk to the well diggers. This whole project seems to be taking a lot of time."

Boukari is carrying a bucket of the provisional rain water to her bathroom. She follows him out to the yard where Augustin is conferring with the workers. She asks for bath water. In the evening, after he heats the water, she'll wash her hair.

That evening, her hair wet, she lingers while drying herself. Her robe and towel are coarse from being line dried in the sun, and she pulls the towel pleasingly across her back in a sawing motion. Hearing clapping and then a knock at her front door she wraps the towel around her hair, pulls on her robe, takes up the lantern and goes to the door. Dressed in a white embroidered smock, bold against the darkness behind him, Augustin stands with a calabash of sagabo. Stepping back, Thea says, "But I've eaten already."

"But I haven't. I thought you might like to taste the sagabo with my own meat sauce," he smiles. This is not their routine. He has never purposely come to see her at night. She feels the weakness in her knees as she greets him with a kiss to each cheek.

"Come in and sit while I change. I hope you left the okra out because it's too slimy for me."

After she changes into her yellow shift, they sit in the kitchen where they had talked for so long waiting on word about Rasmata. She releases her damp hair and lifts it with her fingers. At first she watches as he eats, then she cups her fingers as he does to dip some of the sagabo in the meat sauce. She takes a sip of water and nods, "Yes, I like it, especially with the peppers, but that's all I want for tonight." She waves her hand in front of her mouth to cool it. He picks out another small piquant pepper for her. She takes it into her mouth from his fingers. He leaves them on her lips longer than needed.

She pours water over her hands at the sink and lathers them, never having eaten the sagabo as he does without cutlery. He stands closely behind her as she washes, running his own fingers under the water she pours. She feels his breath on her neck.

They dry their hands on the same towel. Thea is aware of her own breathing. She turns and leans into him.

She leads him to a darker, wider space near the front door. "We haven't talked," she says, her voice weak. "About loving each other. . ."

"I love you, Talato. Marry me and make this your home."

"I want to marry you. I love you. But I really need to tell my family and the church about my situation. It wouldn't be fair to them or to you either, for me to feel so obligated and torn." she says.

"Will you lend me the money to get to Seattle and back?"

"Yes, yes. I understand your need to go.

Talato let me touch you..." His hand is flat against her abdomen, slightly tugging up her skirt as he kisses her. He kneels and uses both hands to pull up her dress. Stretching the cloth of her panty to one side he kisses her. She pulls at the curly tufts of his hair as he carefully spreads the lips of her vagina. Thea tilts backward slightly to comply. With his finger he rubs her briefly. "Like silk," he says.

In the bedroom, Augustin lifts the net over her bed. Thea steps back, wanting to see him in the lantern's light. As she looks she also finds him with her hands. She leans to kiss his taut stomach, smoothing his inner thigh, lightly brushing the tip of his erection, touching the pearl of wetness with the back of her hand.

He lifts her onto the sheet and the shadows of her parted legs splay against the wall. She experiences what she has only imagined and climaxes as he touches her again, massaging her as he kisses her mouth.

Augustin groans as he penetrates still finding her mouth. She arches against him, and climaxes once more while he moves in her, like ocean waves, mounting blue, crashing white. His breathing, deep and long, sounds like the ocean shore, like the tide in a rocky cove. When they kiss again, their mouths are cool.

They talk in the darkness and lie together until nearly dawn. Their comingled scents along with the hints of *Joy* and *Vetiver* they wear linger. He slips down in the narrow bed and uses his tongue to please her until she cries out in a newly found ecstasy. She puts her fingers in the nap of his hair and pulls his face up and into her neck. She rocks him and feels the wet warmth of his tear against her cheek. A rooster crows—already morning.

APPARITIONS

Late morning, a Saturday, Thea sees Augustin at the well. He has sent different men to dig more deeply, hoping for less silt. The pair of diggers is slick with red mud. Another pair in short pants makes bricks of the clay they bring up from the well, laying them in rows in the sun to dry. Thea's yard is full of workers going and coming. They break and stand around the rusty blue barrel being used as a pulpit.

Rows of wet brick lie in her yard, indicative of how much further the workers have dug. She hopes they can be used for her wall. The well diggers pull up a bucket to show Augustin the results of their digging. Augustin cups the water in his hands. "Good work, but we're still not deep enough," he says and instructs one of them to bring Thea a bucket. She swirls the water and the yellow mud coats her hand. "Closer to rock," he says.

There is more digging to be done. Thea knows an improved well is a gift to her.

On Sunday, Sidabé and Thea succeed as usual at drawing a crowd. When no room is left among those seated in the shade, onlookers skirt the zandi. Again, Thea reads Jesus' words from St. John, "No man shall come unto the Father but by me." She reads words she doubts as if to buck up her own spirit. She reads more of Jesus' words further in St. John, "I am the truth, the life, the way." To herself, she thinks: *either we're all God's children or none of us are.*

Though the new converts have heard the song before, no one attempts to sing along when Thea and Sidabé sing "A mighty fortress is our God." The song is long, and the old accordion, left over from another missionary, wheezes back and forth, heavy and cumbersome. Sidabé preaches earnestly for an hour. How can they know who is truly converted? Is there such a word as fortress in either Moore or Fulfulde?

In the audience are little boys with distended stomachs and protruding navels who look like the pictures she saw twenty-one years ago age six, when she responded to being called.

Now, under the zandi, someone picks up his drum, and the cadence of the tribal music begins. Everyone stirs to settle in. The onlookers tighten the circle. Sidabé seats himself comfortably in the circle and enters in with his bass voice, swaying back and forth. Thea packs up her accordion and leaves discreetly. The church is being established.

In the brilliant light of an early Saturday afternoon, three young Mossis arrive with a donkey pulling a two-wheeled cart, its cargo a young Fulani tied down with ropes. He is hunched, his hands holding his head, straining against the ropes. The little grey donkey, his back dusty and scraped, guided by a stick, pulls into Thea's yard dipping his head against the load, stalling before they reach the front door. One of the Mossis in traditional garb comes to her door, clapping loudly. Norogo has come for a soda and sees them from his vantage point beneath the zandi. He hurries forward, always ready to be of help. Boukari is stooped, sweeping the yard. He stands, transfixed by what he sees.

"They have found a crazy person at the lorry stop and they want you to pray for him," Norogo translates.

Measuring the impact of one's presence is impossible. Removing one's self from the scene and knowing what might have transpired is beyond imagination. Thea wonders what would occur here in this village had she not come.

Who can weigh the difference one makes? Who can know one's impact on a person, a household or a whole village? She hesitates not wanting to spur the rumor that her prayers reach God. Is she doing some good or has she disrupted a way of life in an irreversible manner? Is she interfering or is she helping? She has too little life experience to know the answers. She feels confused, her mind like a murky well she can't draw from.

Confounded, she prays, putting her hand on the Fulani's back, wet with perspiration, smelling strongly of body odor and fear, his white cotton shirt torn in a ragged line from sun exposure and sheer wear. She prays in English without Norogo translating. Her voice soothes him, and he becomes still as he crouches beneath the ropes, his shoulders relaxing.

The Mossis have an excited exchange. Then they watch silently, standing away from the cart. The donkey shifts its weight, tilting the well-worn cart, flicking his ears back. Everything is quiet. Thea lets her hand rest on the Fulani's shoulder and continues to pray. She wonders what has transpired, an effectual prayer or a reaction to her touch and a soft, female voice. She begins to loosen the ties, and he looks into her face. She sees a child/man, with hope in his gaze.

The Mossis explain he came off a lorry from Ouagadougou acting as if he were having apparitions. He struggled with the men, resisting their efforts to help him. The young Fulani has probably been deported from Abidjan, Ivory Coast, where more than likely he became addicted to cocaine. They tell her the fate of others they have known who have gone illegally to Abidjan to work, who were given cocaine by their employers so they would work harder, and deported when thin and exhausted, put on the train to Ouagadougou with no one to receive them on the other end. Now, they explain he is more than likely reacting to his withdrawal. Probably recognizing him as a Fulani, someone had put him on a truck to Kongoussi.

Thea sees a young Fulani out of his depth in another culture, someone who needs his family. Once loosed from the cart, she and Norogo lead him to the shade of the zandi. She unrolls a grass mat and he lies down, his hands under his head. He is thin, but fit and strong. His skin is chalky and grey with dirt. He has no belongings.

Boukari sets a pail of filtered water next to the newcomer who sits up and drinks from his cupped hands. Boukari continues sweeping the yard until it looks combed, looking uneasily to the scene of Thea and the Fulani. He appears wary of the newcomer.

The young man answers Norogo's questions readily but shows his respect by not looking at either Thea or Norogo directly. If he lifts his head, it is to look north into the distance.

They learn his name is Ibrahima, Abraham. He is fifteen. When questioned, he talks of reuniting with his parents in the bush, certain he can find them in the desert because they will be herding their cattle on the same route they have used since his childhood. His thinking seems clear.

By custom, at fifteen, it is time for him to take charge of a herd for a three-month period to complete his rite of passage. After his experience in the outside world, he tells Norogo he is now ready to be tested by his family and tribe by driving the migration of a herd on the ancient routes and bringing them back healthy.

Thea realizes he wouldn't survive if he walked home. He has no place to go for the night, interprets Norogo. Ibrahima allows Thea to tend the rope burns on his arms and back, while she considers what to do.

Augustin comes at his usual hour. Thea's lesson in Moore has been deferred, and she finishes quickly as he rides in, more than anxious to talk with him about her afternoon. Ibrahima sleeps near one of the poles of the zandi.

Thea speaks to Augustin, "Some young men from the market tied him into a donkey cart and brought him here for me to pray for." Augustin listens carefully to both her account and Norogo's longer one.

"I think we should help him find his parents," Norogo says, volunteering his advice, scuffing the zekka lightly with his sandal.

"This is common among boys his age, both Mossi and Fulani. They're torn between two lives." Augustin says. Let me see the Commandant in Kaya about his Landrover.

While Augustin goes to search him out, Thea prepares her usual tiresome fare, still afraid to try the fly covered beef hanging in the market.

She knows she can't take in the full significance of Ibrahim's choice to return home. How agonizing for him to leave in the first place before undergoing his rite of passage. When he returns home, will they kill the fatted calf or will they turn him away? How few, the choices for a young man from a desert tribe. No one had taken into account his innocence. Rather they had abused him and taken advantage of his body's youth and strength.

Augustin returns after sunset, and after kissing in the privacy of the kitchen, they go directly to the zandi. "Salaamu Aleykum," he greets Ibrahima. Norogo stays to interpret. Thea presents the sagabo, leaving the lantern so Norogo and Ibrahima can eat privately.

"Do you feel afraid of him spending the night under the zandi if Norogo can stay? I'll check with Norogo before I go. I've brought Ibrahima a shirt and found a place for him to stay tomorrow night."

"What about the clinic?"

"I've arranged to be off. I can rent the Landrover from the Commandant to take him home. The elders at the market say he can point the way." Augustine and Thea hold each other briefly inside before Thea lights another lantern. Their longing fills the darkening night.

"Shall I come back when everything is quiet?"

"*Beogo*," she responds. Tomorrow.

Ibrahima stays overnight under the zandi. Norogo, ever willing, stays with him. Thea listens from her bed as Ibrahima and Norogo talk into the night. Thea doesn't know until morning that Boukari stays as well, seemingly intent on protecting her.

Before dawn Augustin brings a baguette. Thea prepares coffee with sweetened condensed milk, and they sit under the zandi looking to the sun, rising like a golden coin on the far horizon. Ibrahima is still curled in the blankets, head covered.

Later, Ibrahima is in the healing line behind the deaf/mute who comes daily. Freshly bathed and in his new shirt, he waits for her prayer. As Norogo translates she prays for help finding Ibrahima's home. She feels him tremble. He feels clammy but remains calm. He seems especially thirsty.

The next evening, Augustin comes to her, but they make no noise. At one point, they muffle their laughter in Thea's favorite quilt. He slips away, and she can't sleep for her longing.

The next morning Norogo tells those waiting to be prayed for that Thea and Augustin are taking Ibrahima home. "God be your help," they concur, breaking out of the line, having water before they go.

Augustin arrives in the Landrover with two gallons of filtered water and enough food, ready to begin their journey into the vast reaches of the Sahel, to find Ibrahima's barukka in the desert. Ibrahima will judge by the time of the year where his family will be in their migratory route. He will know how to find the water holes. He will know their cattle when he sees them.

Ibrahima points the way across the barren terrain, sitting forward in the seat, looking over the hood of the Landrover, the color of cardboard. The windows closed, the dust still comes through the vents, blowing in their faces. Riding in the back seat, Thea finds it hard to breathe. Augustin stops the Landrover. She vomits into the stubbles of grass. They have passed most of the vegetation, and all that lies before them is an expanding plain of dirty sand and small stands of twisted, gnarled trees. The plain ahead shimmers like a dark lake, a mirage, like an unfolded canvas.

They travel for three hours. Around the water holes the cattle are allowed to graze until the grass is gone and the earth is torn up before going on to the next wadi.

Thea can't hold down water, so they stop under a stand of pale green, warped brush. She leans over, her head in her hands until the nausea passes. The thorny, sparsely leaved brush offers little shade.

Later, under such a stand, they find Ibrahima's family. The barukka is the same color as the earth, nearly camouflaged. Ibrahima leans forward, pressing his head against the windshield, his hands behind him clutching the seat. A white rooster shoots across the yard, frightened by the rover. Thea sees the man who must be Ibrahima's father run to a pole near the hut. He switches his white cap to one embroidered with several colors and walks toward them, his long caftan disguising the slimness belied by his thin shoulders. Ibrahima leaps out the door.

The father is hesitant at first; then recognizing his oldest son, they embrace. They sway together with the embrace. Ibrahima's father pushes him back and turns to show Ibrahima to his mother who stands with her hands spread against her cheeks. Other children stand very still near the door of the barukka.

The scene seems surreal to Thea, and tears well and stream down her pallid cheeks.

"*Useka, useka,*" thank you, thank you, they repeat as they embrace their son. "Thank God who is merciful?"

The father instructs a younger brother to catch the rooster, and he scurries after the squawking chicken, running back and forth across the yard until it is caught and tied. Augustin accepts the rooster, but before they go, Ibrahima's mother leads Thea into the hut and presents three round balls of precious hand-made soap. They feel heavy. Thea brought no gifts.

How could Thea think to tell these people their souls are in jeopardy unless they accept Jesus as their Lord? She is defeated by her compassion before she has begun. It seems her experiences in this strange land have undermined all she believed. Now that God is a stranger, she has a deepened sense of respect for others.

On their way back, Augustin rests his hand on Thea's knee. They have placed a carton over the clucking, struggling rooster. It goes quiet. She leans into his shoulder as the sun sets, and the long day descends into night. The temperature drops. Augustin stops and reaches for a heavy, hand-woven cotton throw, placing it over her knees and around her shoulder. She tips into his lap and falls asleep as he retraces their journey, checking his compass as they go.

She wakens to his hands in her hair, his fingers threading through the strands around her neck. She runs her hand beneath his shirt, finding and caressing the nipple. He stops under the cloak of night.

"Talato," he says. She hears her name like a lost child being called. She answers by finding his lips with her fingers, meeting them with her mouth. The hallowed silence, the star-pierced darkness, and the hovering passion between them are gifts of the night, perhaps from the universe, or God himself.

★★★★

As they drive into Thea's yard Norogo is asleep in the zandi. Immediately he rushes to carry the cooler and the water inside. "You found Ibrahima's home?"

"Yes, but why aren't you home?" She asks in a rather maternal way, belying her affection for him. His determination to fill a need is at once an asset and a deficit. She fears he doesn't take enough time with his family, especially now with Araba in his thoughts.

Thea makes coffee. They sit under the zandi while Augustin describes their trip to Norogo: the hyenas they saw in route coming home; the Fulanis and water holes they found, surrounded by milling herds of long horned cattle. In the retelling of the reunion, Augustin is reminded of the rooster beneath the carton. He offers it to Norogo to take to his family. "It's your namesake," he adds. "Norogo means rooster, after all."

Sleepily, Thea's mind wanders away from the conversation. Closing her eyes, she thinks of home. She has not lived independently before coming to Kongoussi. There has always been a dorm, a rental, a stranger for a roommate.

Home with her parents is on the Columbia River, so close to its mouth that they experience the tides of the Pacific Ocean. Its silver waters run rich with salmon, sturgeon, steelhead and smelt. Great stands of timber--- cedar, fir, spruce and alder--- border the fields where Thea has spent many hours on the ranch feeding the cattle, raking and baling hay. White-tailed deer can be seen in the evening grazing on the edge of the cleared pastures. She drives often around the dike at dusk just to view them at a distance.

Norogo slips away quietly. The rooster continues to stretch its neck to peck at him as he carries it away upside down.

"In America the Northwestern sun is slow to rise and slow to set," She says, her eyes still closed, putting her thoughts to words. "Sometimes the sun shows through a thin haze of clouds, but usually the clouds cover the actual sphere of the sun. It's so unlike this equatorial place where night falls almost unexpectedly, and the intense heat comes with sunrise."

"Are you missing your homeland?" He asks, stretching to rake his hand against her cheek. A soft rain sifts through the zandi. When she begins to drift into sleep, he guides her to bed, and she sleeps in a rainbow's light until noon.

UNTANGLED

Augustin drives to Ouagadougou the following Saturday to purchase Thea's ticket to Seattle. Thea doesn't go because he has other business to tend to in the city. She plans to fly Air France from Ouagadougou to Niamey, Mali on to Paris. From Paris she'll take United Airlines on the polar route over the vast desert of arctic ice to home.

Augustin returns, and she hears the Peugeot drive up. He brings a cooler with beef tenderloin, vegetables she hasn't seen for a while, and tiny strawberries. In a box from the French bakery, he presents a chocolate-filled cream puff and a croissant for her breakfast. They eat the sweet strawberries in the kitchen standing side by side, and she laughs for the pleasure of it, remembering having imagined them eating a mango together. He hands her the ticket, and she draws a breath that catches in her throat.

"I don't want to be away from you. You *are* a healer. You've healed me and saved me both. I felt so lost before you came, lost and jaded." he says, leaning his head into her shoulder.

Augustin is not rushed in their lovemaking. He satisfies her with his sensitive fingers while she massages his erection. She mounts him, her hands planted on his chest; breathing rapidly, she arches her back to receive him. Later, he sleeps against her and she draws the sheet over him, touching his graying temple, tracing his spine with her hand. Her touch interrupts the breathing of his sleep. She is more careful to resist touching him. A soft rain falls on the tin roof and purls through the eaves, trickling into the rain barrel. The magic and the mystery, a sense of the spiritual bathe her. She is quiet with it, quiet with loving him.

They know the village is astir, speculating about their future as a couple. Augustin Quedrago descends from horsemen who, in about 1500, rode into the basin of the White Volta River and conquered farmers in the north. Considered a noble, he must have concerns, Thea thinks, about his status among the villagers. The antipathy of the elders and Chief could hinder his work at the clinic. If they approve, so will the village.

The Mossis carefully pass down their history by word of mouth, the Father telling his sons and daughter's tales of conquest from the 14th century forward. Though many stories have been told with young and old alike surrounding their evening fire, much remains to be conveyed to Augustin's children and grandchildren. She worries about interrupting these patterns; she worries about their acceptance of her. His sons and their wives are very formal with her on the occasions she is invited into their large compound, but the children pull their stools close-by, and the eldest son keeps her glass full.

"You mustn't choose me over them." she says.

"You can be there and listen too. Someday, you may have to tell the stories. "

Thea thinks and talks of making the trip home. She arranges for work to begin on a six-foot mud wall to be built around the compound, hoping by the time she is back, the project will have been accomplished. People coming to her will be required to ask permission to enter her yard. Privacy has never been as important to her.

She hears the ringing of the shovels as the well diggers strike rock. The water is clear. For a time, Boukari is busy filling the containers that onlookers bring to share in the celebration.

With the bricks that are dried and ready to be placed the workers begin building walls inside the well, excited and chatting, one handing down mortar, another handing down bricks. They call Thea to hand down the last brick.

They take turns gouging out foot holds in the wet mortar down to the level of the rock and come diving up, sputtering and flailing, grinning and being congratulated on their work. Thea's heart is here among the celebrants, she knows, as the disturbed water settles. She sees that the well will become a resource and decides not to wall it off.

On Sunday Sidabé and she have the usual crowd of converts who come regularly to the Sunday service. People continue to crowd on the periphery while the service is being conducted. The air is hot and close. Sidabé preaches against the sacrifice of chickens to the ancestors, of goats to the spirits. He walks back and forth in front of the barrel pulpit, Norogo close at his elbow, while Thea sits in one of the two chairs, with her accordion, more of its purple luster faded and lost to the sun, propped on the zekka beside her.

Sidabé asks for new converts and they sing a chorus he has taught them. "My heart is happy, now that I know Jesus." They sing loudly, clapping in rhythm. One of the older women in the front leads out with a verse in a minor key. The others repeat the words together, leaning into their tambourines and over the drums, as they voluntarily make the transition from Sidabé's new music to their own, creating the words as they are inspired.

Sidabé is an authentic, humble man, also fervent. While he asks for a show of hands of those who want salvation, Thea picks up her accordion and plays the song she has often heard being played to set the tone during an altar call, even though those for whom she plays don't know the words: "*Just as I am without one plea, but that thy blood was shed for me; Just as I am and waiting not, to rid my soul of one dark blot. I come."*

Her own soul feels the familiar seduction she felt as a girl. She had often answered altar calls as this song was sung until her father told her that one time was sufficient. She had felt it hard to resist the pull, the drawing by the Holy Spirit, she thought of as the very voice of God.

"The supreme sacrifice has been made by Jesus, the Lamb of God," Sidabé explains. "God no longer expects sacrifices of goats, sheep and chicken."

Three young Mossis in traditional clothes come forward to accept the *good news*. Watching them in their sincerity, hands held straight to their sides, heads bowed, Thea feels regret and loss that she no longer believes what she came to tell.

As on every Sunday, numbers are added. Norogo is eager to interpret all the nuances of their testimonies and does so capably. Their offerings are generous. The service stretches on into the afternoon.

Augustin has never appeared on Sunday, but he comes later that afternoon when the congregation and onlookers have gone, the zekka swept and cleared.

Thea says to him as they walk toward the kitchen, "The saying goes that some are Christian, some are Muslim, but all are animists. We have no way of knowing they have abandoned their old beliefs for Christianity. They still wear their fetishes and gris gris."

"I don't think you will ever know. We can never know the true beliefs of another, never mind our own. We often don't know our *own* beliefs, Talato. Some of our inner perceptions have never been articulated, and we don't know our own subconscious biases until a situation presents its self and we have to make choices. When we begin to sort it out, we see the fundamental notions of our own beliefs and their influence on us.

As they invest themselves, this little church will grow and become what they need it to become. It's beautiful to watch how they are coming to care about each other. What they really believe, even if it's a mixture of beliefs doesn't really matter in my opinion. The premise is almost beside the point. Knowing and loving God may be an unrealistic notion, but pursued by most of us as you know."

When the door is closed, they embrace. "The way you and I love each other is unique and feels spiritual to me," she says quietly against his shirt. She toys with an embroidered sleeve, rubbing the intricately sewn threads between her fingers.

"Thea, though we can never completely know each other, I think our love surmounts any notions about knowing. I hold our love sacred, cherishing the part of you I do know, the soul I've touched on."

Thea responds, "I've always separated the carnal, 'the things of the flesh' as St. Paul called them, from the spiritual. It's as if I've been two persons. Oswald Chambers, the author of a devotional I was using, says to deny the carnal aspects of self. Now, I'm indulging them and feel freed.

It's as if I have had to choose whether to deny my love for you and admit I don't have a gospel to tell or leave you altogether for the outward preservation of what others see as my faith in Jesus as the only way to God. I no longer have faith in the God I thought I knew.

God isn't who they told me they thought He was. I used to pray King David's Psalm that says 'Unite my heart to fear thy name' because I've always been torn between two selves. I was taught from a child that I was born a sinner. I'm finding it hard to look at the world any other way. A sinner saved by grace."

Continuing, she says, "Look at these people who believe I have a special connection with God. How can I live among them with you unless I concede to them that their God is also my God? While I was out with the Fulanis in the moonlight, the mystery of the universe and its infinity was so apparent to me, that I question if I have the right to define the God of the universe for someone else. I've spent my life studying and preparing for this mission. Now I find I can't fulfill what I have held onto for my lifetime: a calling by God to be a Christian missionary. I've fallen in love with you...

The people who support me back home have a right to know that. I've things to say to my parents and my supporters I can't say in letters."

Thea can't conceive the reactions if she were to tell them of her intentions to return and marry Augustin. But, to be true to herself, she feels she must return and speak openly.

"Go, if you must, *ma Cherie,* but come back to me," he says without hesitation.

Later in the bedroom with no lantern, they inadvertently bring the mosquito net down around them, frame and all. Crawling out, Thea brings a lantern. Augustin's erect penis is tangled and exposed outside the net. They laugh together while she uses the scissors to cut him free. He watches the rescue intently, cautioning her, his shoulders shaking with laughter as she snips.

Thea takes the opportunity to teach him words in English that she wants to hear, that might arouse her at the right moment. "Prick," she says, tweaking him there.

"Preek," he repeats.

"No, prick, prick. Let's try clit.

"Cleet, cleet," he says, touching her teasingly.

Laughing, she knows she'll not be stimulated by these words in their lovemaking. She'll only be made to laugh.

MOONSTONES

Later that week Thea visits Moise, the tailor, in the market. She passes the lean, fly-covered carcasses hanging at the meat market where the vultures prance, advancing and retreating over the discarded entrails.

A man she's not seen before approaches her as she looks at the tomatoes. Strips of rags are tied to his body in bulky layers. His thin shoulders are bare. Limping haltingly toward her with a stick, he holds his dry, withered hand in front of Thea. She looks into his face and sees a demanding, angry fire in his eyes. His papery face is uncomfortably close. She smells the excrement on his rags. Repulsed and frightened, she meets his eyes again. Beggars should be humble she thinks and is immediately ashamed that she feels no compassion. The vender shoos him away. Thea feels the momentary loss of her normal compassionate response like a lost jewel, something irreplaceable.

Moise sits under the veranda of a white-washed concrete block building treadling his shiny black and gold antique Singer sewing machine, the Mercedes Benz of sewing machines. Machine embroidered shirts and tops hang about him and overhead. She brings an example of a summer dress she wants him to copy. She begins to choose, feeling the fabric from among the many bolts stacked up in the semi-darkness of the room behind him. She senses someone's presence and looks up to find Abdul.

Abdul is thin, dirty, poorly dressed, with one shoulder bare, his hair long, dusty and spongy. Thea embraces him. "Boukari told me you were in the market. Rasmata prepared a gift for you while she was in labor," he says. "I wanted to give it to you before you go."

They walk together to his old bike where he pulls out a small package. When she unties the string and opens the scrap of brown paper, she finds beads of moonstone, white, translucent, slightly blue, like skim milk, like opals. She cups them and stirs them with one finger.

She stands quietly for a moment. They remind her of the opaque light of the moon out among the Fulani cattle, how transformed she was in the depth of the silence as if God himself were showing her how undefinable he is. The silence that night was broken by the piercing yet breathy sound of the flute, and the disconsolate notes had stirred her blood for Augustin. Spiritual and sensual in the same moment, her awareness of a God profound, her need for Augustin heightened, she felt changed. The moonstones are the perfect reminder of Rasmata and the trembling, life-changing transition Thea made from one belief to another.

"*Baraka, Baraka wousego,*" Thank you very much, she says to Abdul. "I can never forget Rasmata. She truly loved you," Thea says.

"The way you love Augustin?" he asks.

"Yes, the way I love Augustin." Thea confesses.

"Abdul," she adds, "Rasmata would want you to ride the new moped."

WHAT IS AND HAS BEEN

The crowded airport is guarded by armed soldiers. They bar the insistent beggars from entering and tell them to go back to the mosque where Muslims are required to give alms to the poor. They make way for Augustin and Thea to pass. Augustin and Thea wait for the delayed Air France flight in the hot, stale air of Gate One's departure zone. Before Thea boards, Augustin briefly holds her for the first time in a public place. "Talato," he says. "I love you. Come back soon." He climbs the stairs to the upper deck to watch her go.

"*Je reviens*," she promises. I'll be back.

Onboard, the air is close, and she reaches for the vent above her head. No air yet. The passengers wait for over an hour on the tarmac. She thinks of Augustin waiting for the plane to leave. If her connection goes well in Paris, she'll be in Seattle, nearly home in Cathlamet, in less than twenty four hours.

In Southwest Washington, an old trading post, Cathlamet sits on a rugged bluff overlooking the Columbia River in Wahkiakum County, the broad tidal estuary near the mouth of the Columbia. It was once the largest village of the Wahkiakum Indians west of the Cascades. When sighted in1792 while verifying Captain Robert Gray's discovery of the Columbia River, it had three to four hundred Indians living in cedar homes.

Lewis and Clark spent the night there sleeplessly, complaining of the dampness.

The fur traders brought diseases, and by the late 1830's the Wahkiakum tribe was decimated. Many died of measles or other diseases that came with the immigrants. In 1846, James Birnie, with his ten children, became the first white settler, and real change began. His sister, Charlotte, became the first school teacher.

In time, the remaining disenfranchised Indians retreated to other locations on the Columbia. A white spired church visible from the river was built in 1895, dominating Main Street. In 1938 the Julia Butler Hansen Bridge was built across the Columbia River's Cathlamet channel to Puget Island, which had become home for Norwegians, Swedes and various others, tending their Holstein or Jersey cattle on its verdant fields. From the hills beyond one could see their red barns surrounded by the green pastures, dotted with herds of Holstein, Guernsey or Jerseys.

Fishermen made their catches on the Columbia and parked their boats next to their homes in the diked sloughs snaking through the island. Often they left their families and went to Alaska for the summer to take advantage of the rich salmon run in its deep cold waters.

The loggers lived mostly in the fertile, green Elochoman Valley through which the rushing Elochoman River weaves its way to the Columbia, bringing melted snow off the mountains. At one time a narrow gauge railroad traced the route of the river down the mountain to the log depot. Early on, one rail car would often hold just one log of virgin timber, hundreds of years old. The sound, like a thrashing machine, and the shrill whistle undid the silence of the valley. Loggers in short pants and heavy boots swung out the sides as they crossed the intersections waving at the children who stood at the crossroads.

Small, identical, temporary houses on skids made up a family camp of loggers at the end of the paved road into the valley, and housed fifty or more families. The children were called *camp kids* in school when Thea was of school age.

Now, Cathlamet's Main Street is lined with empty storefronts. Its docks are used by small fishing vessels, tugboats and recreational boats. As a girl, she remembers clearly, it was a busy town: two taverns, a theatre, two grocery stores, two clothing stores, a dime store, a liquor store, a dry cleaner, a hardware store, and two filling stations with the cold grape pop she craved in deep tin coolers. She remembers the drug store where she and her mother ate warm cashews and had chocolate sodas. When Crown Zellerbach closed down, having finished clearing the virgin timber and moved its logging operations elsewhere, even the shoemaker, who specialized in logging boots, went broke.

Matt, her father, is a successful rancher, raising a breed of registered Shorthorns. His handsome, husky beef, a deep umber, bred to have no horns, graze on the tide lands created by diking the Columbia. Prized newborn calves come in the spring, and fattened steers go to market in the fall. He has done well with his fifth grade education and his instincts about cattle rearing.

Her parents' conversion to Christianity occurred when Thea was two. One of her first memories is of the small New Testament her father carried everywhere, its soft black leather binding holding Jesus' words in red letters. For him it was the inspired word of God. He was twenty nine. He stopped smoking and started chewing Doublemint gum. Her mother stopped using red lipstick. She was twenty-six.

At six, sitting on the front row of the River of Life Christian Church beside her best friend, Thea responded to a *calling* to be in the ministry.

At nine she and her parents were awarded an attendance pen for seven years without missing Sunday school. Her father's faithfulness was rewarded, and he soon became chairman of the board. When the decision was made to erect a new church, he dedicated himself to building it.

Her mother, Lilly, began teaching Sunday school to primary girls soon after she was converted and continued through the years, cutting out the figures for the flannel graph on Saturday nights: Moses parting the Red Sea; John the Baptist baptizing Jesus; or making a diorama out of a shoe box of Lazarus being resurrected from the grave.

Thea knew no other life than going to church, ranching, going to school. She wasn't allowed to go to movies or to dance. At nine, she read *The Yearling* by Marjorie Rawlings and wanted a fawn of her own. She read all the *Nancy Drew* books and wanted to solve mysteries. She read *Black Beauty* by Anne Sewell and wanted a horse, which she received when she was 12. She read *The Thundering Herd* by Zane Gray and wanted adventure. Books were the magic in her life.

Her affections were focused on her father, as were Lilly's. When he was in the process of building a garage or an out-building, Thea anticipated what he needed, handing him two by fours, a saw, a hammer, a plane or six-penny nails one at a time. She loved the smell of fresh lumber and toying with the blonde curls from the boards he planed. Lily swept up the sawdust around him as he worked.

She remembers how he played his guitar sometimes in the evening, and in his tenor voice he played and sang Bill Gorgan's Goat if she begged:

> *Bill Gorgan's goat was feeling fine,*
> *Ate three red shirts right off the line.*
> *Bill took a stick,*
> *Gave him three whacks*
> *And tied him to the railroad tracks.*
> *The whistle blew.*
> *The train drew nigh.*

Bill Gorgan's goat
Was doomed to die.
He gave three groans of awful pain,
Coughed up the shirts
And flagged the train.

"Again, again," Thea would beg when she was very small.

Thea learned to drive the now nearly retired tractor, Betsy, at ten. As a teen, she raked and baled twenty tons of hay each summer, her friend Sheila sometimes riding on the side of the tractor with her. Now she is coming home in July during haying season. Without the projection of a three-day hiatus in the normal rainy patterns, the hay can't be cut. If too damp, the hay must be tedded, turned from the swath and scattered for drying several times before being baled. She wonders about the weather report and remembers those times on the tractor, circling the field looking toward her future, compelled to go to Africa. It was God's will. She was certain.

The congregants of the little church are committed, coming on Sunday evenings for a vesper service as well as Wednesday evenings for Bible study. Among the congregation are many Scandinavians, Norwegians, Finns and Swedes with old world accents, working as fishermen, farmers and loggers. Thea tries to place Augustin in this setting, his color, his accent, his other-world ways. She cannot.

Thea's ties to the land, to her parents to her church fellow-ship, to her friends are strong and had been uncomplicated. There's the special Ragna Rodahl, an elderly Norwegian lady with a strong brogue. Thea's parents have picked her up for church for years. She's attended all of Thea's events from eighth grade graduation to her ordination. If Thea greets her with the conventional: 'May the Lord bless you,' she responds, "He do, He do." She is much shorter than Thea and when they embrace she comes to Thea's chest.

Thea fingers the beads from Rasmata, who taught her how to dance, remembering being received in her compound, remembering the babies she had tended so competently, her role in the changes in the Fulani community's attitude toward medicine. She thinks back to Ouaihagouya and Rasmata's success there. She thinks of their friendship, wishing now she could talk to her about loving Augustin, someone from another culture like Rasmata's Abdul.

She thinks of Norogo, his ability to quickly learn what is needed, his eagerness to do it. Hado, from the prayer line comes to mind. His leg is regaining strength after extracting the guinea worm. He comes now to bring her gifts, a chicken or a guinea fowl. Norogo redistributes the many other gifts she receives to needy villagers. She thinks of others in the daily prayer line and the seemingly miraculous recovery of some, the sad loss of others.

During the seven night time hours to Paris, she authenticates her love for Augustin by imagining his ways, especially his ways with her, the gentle, careful hands; the gentle, careful heart, her wakened passion, her changed perspective. She notices an African making his way down the aisle. For a second she thinks it is Augustin, and her heart constricts.

Thea retrieves her luggage in Paris and the complicated connection between Paris and Seattle goes well. Feeling ragged and unrested, she lands in Seattle, early afternoon on a clear day. Below her she can see Mount Rainier. She sees the glacial ice glistening in the sunlight; Puyallup River Valley stretching out like a tapestry, the Cascades cradling the city of Seattle, Elliot Bay busy with ferries, like crawling beetles, the Space Needle from the World's Fair of 1962.

Her father, Matt, with his long stride reaches her before her mother. They are overcome, not speaking, just embracing. "You must have brought the sunshine with you," he finally says. He is dressed in a suit and tie.

Thea reaches for her mother whispering, "I love you." Her mother dabs Thea's face and her own with a lace handkerchief, a faint and familiar scent of Purex on her hands. She uses the embroidered corner and carefully, tenderly wipes beneath Thea's eyelashes.

Thea sleeps the two hours from Seattle on I-5 until they reach Longview, a city that perpetually smells of the pulp mills on the river front. From there they wind twenty miles along the Columbia River to Cathlamet. She sits up and puts aside the plaid, Pendleton car blanket her mother has pulled over her.

Ships come from the Pacific, through the rough seas of the bar that riffle over the banks of sand in the mouth of the river. Along this drive from Longview to Cathlamet, their cargo steams up the river from Astoria, Oregon, and glides through the channel in route to Portland. Thea remembers waving to them from her tractor seat, answering a call of sorts to be going somewhere exotic. She wishes she could take this mighty river to the desert and direct its course across the Sub-Sahel.

She watches for the familiar waterfalls on her right flowing from the rocky face of the timbered escarpment, remembering how as a child she thought of Moses smiting and splitting the rock in the wilderness with his rod, the water gushing out to quench the thirst of the people. She wishes for her girlhood, how uncomplicated it was, how simple the way to redemption, how plausible the miracles. But, she thinks, how shallow her well has been, how narrowed and abbreviated her pursuit of knowledge.

Seeing she is awake in the rear view mirror, Matt turns off the gospel music playing on the eight track tape recorder in their new Buick. He loosens his tie. They begin talking, and he tells her of the sudden and recent death of Ragna, the petite Norwegian of whom Thea is so fond. She was a friend and an integral part of Thea's childhood. Thea feels the loss as she watches the river flow by. Rasmata had such a short life, she thinks, by comparison.

He reports the Puget Islanders are having success with their cucumbers, a cash crop they sell in gunny bags to Nalley's by the truck load; Sheila, her best friend, is looking forward to seeing her, as is everyone. He goes on, her mother adding to or detracting from his accounts.

They drive home, along Steamboat Slough where the stubs of the velvet brown cattails crowd the tall grass.

They have no television and her parents play Chinese checkers quietly in the kitchen over coffee while she sleeps in her old room, surrounded by the artifacts of her youth: a volley ball trophy, a tennis racket, a clarinet, her books and old texts, her saddle, the Elvis Presley records, the white Bible she was given at graduation from eighth grade. A copy of a waif with great mournful eyes holding what must be a stray cat hangs on the wall.

Her texts and commentaries fill a bottom shelf and commemorate a long journey through seminary and into the ministry. The air is fresh, and there are no sounds except the deep-voiced bull frogs croaking along the slough. The pillow case is ironed as well as the border of the sheet. With no reminders except the emptiness in her heart, she brings an imagined Augustin into her arms, smothering her face in her down pillow before falling into a hard sleep.

In the morning, Matt, in his white bib apron, makes pancakes and eggs, and she pours the warm maple syrup from Canada over the buttered stack he sets in front of her. Her mother is methodically cleaning up his "mess."

"Nothing like a good breakfast to start your day," He says, flipping another batch. The bacon is crisp, the eggs over easy. Thea takes in the familiar sound of the percolator and the odor of Folger's and watches them communicate without words. He hands Lilly the emptied bowl and spatula and holds out his mug for more coffee. She pours it to the level he prefers, just where the cup is stained, slightly below the lip.

Late morning, leaning on the antique desk in sharp contrast to the features of the ultra-modern house, her fingers running over the white doily her mother has crocheted, she dials her best friend, Sheila, a petite redhead she has known and loved over her lifetime. For many years they sat together in the same Sunday school class, answered the same altar calls. Spending the night together at Sheila's, they passed many evenings, watching "I Love Lucy (in the chocolate factory), Little House on the Prairie," or "Lassie" on Sunday afternoon. They were disappointed to find there was more than one Lassie acting the part. Sheila's mother made Congo Squares, and they ate them warm during commercials with the chocolate still oozing.

In their girlhood they shared every confidence. Sheila reached puberty before Thea, and Thea remembers she wouldn't agree to spend the night if she had her period. They arrange to meet in the afternoon at the coffee shop under new management, taking over the old struggling one overlooking the river on Main Street.

Sheila has married, had a child and is now divorced. Thea listens again to the story of Bill, her violent husband, the long, gut-wrenching custody battle. The outcome was not in Sheila's favor. Sheila and he share custody, and he pays no alimony. In such a small congregation she carries the stigma of divorce, of being pregnant before marriage as well as being associated with a non-Christian, a drinker, now known to be violent.

Without a college degree or vocational training, she has found work as a nurse's aide in the local Riverview Nursing Home, the old folks' home, a job Thea had taken briefly to help pay her way to school at Seattle Pacific University. Sheila relies on her mother to babysit Madeleine, her baby. She lives in a single wide mobile home in Rosedale on Columbia Highway.

Her parents are dairy farmers who live on Puget Island, always trying to get ahead.

"I feel trapped and alone," she concludes.

"As Maddy gets older, I'm sure it will get better. You have the world, when you have a child. How is your car holding up?"

"My car is leaking oil, and sometimes I think I put more oil in than I do gas. And, no I don't have the world. I've no time for myself. I talk to old people all day."

As always, Thea begins to expose her own heart, realizing its impact. "My life is there now, with Augustin," Thea finishes. "I love Augustin."

"But you've only been there five months," Sheila responds urgently.

Maddy, at eighteen months, toddles around the shop. Her chubby legs take her to the window that looks out over the river. "Water," she says, pointing, patting her fat hands against the glass. A seagull in a sharp dive dips in full view. Others perch on the grayed, splitting pilings.

Sheila scoops Maddy up and jiggles her on her knee while searching for a Sippy cup in the diaper bag. "He's not a Christian?" she ascertains.

With Maddy squirming on Sheila's lap, Thea feels disappointed by the question and is suddenly pressed to leave. She answers cryptically, "It doesn't matter to me."

"How will you tell your parents, Thea? They'll be crushed." Sheila says. Uneasy, Thea looks at her watch and stands to go. More can be said later.

Thea does not deviate from her plan to stay a month, though her parents encourage her otherwise. When Pastor Jacobsen calls and asks her to give the sermon on Sunday morning she agrees and pores over old notes. She pulls her seminary books on sermon writing. Hermeneutics, she recalls, one of her favorite classes.

He calls back and asks her to give the invocation in the native language. She agrees, willing to be a part of the intrigue, glad she has memorized the Lord's Prayer in Moore.

A FRAGILE SILENCE

Matt mows the twenty acres of oats, his familiar, straight-backed figure circling the field. The forecast is for three days of sunshine. If they work hard, they can get the raking and baling done before the weather changes. He'll hire help to load the truck and stack the pungent rectangular bales in the hayloft. Thea will drive the lurching old truck in first gear with its sensitive clutch as they load, trying to ease forward smoothly for the sake of the loaders.

Silently, Thea and Lilly watch him from the window in his bib overalls mounted on the John Deere. Thea will follow with the Case Caterpillar and rake behind him after the cut grass has lain in the sun for a few hours. The fog is beginning to burn off, and large patches of blue sky are visible over the river.

Lilly puts on a pot of beans and salt pork. She rolls out pastry, and Thea slices the apples for pie. Thea bites into a juicy Gravenstein, savoring its tartness. She hesitates for a moment before she drinks cold water from the faucet without filtering or boiling it.

Thea describes the vibrant Rasmata, her success with the starving infants from her own tribe.

"She was like a sister to me," Thea says.

"Would you have liked having a sister?" Lilly asks.

"Very much, "Thea responds. "Mother, I've fallen in love," suddenly changing the subject.

"Is it with this Augustin you talk so much about in your letters?"

"Yes."

Lilly's face clouds. She busies herself fluting the crust to the pie, opening the oven door to check the temperature. Her face is closed as she slides the pie in and sets the timer. She brushes her hands against her apron, not looking Thea in the eye.

Lilly had always expressed she didn't believe there was acceptance of women as ministers. She has told Matt more than once that's the ministry is no place for a woman. She had expressed doubts about Thea succeeding in Africa, simply because she was a woman. Now, apparently, she has failed.

"What does this Augustin do? How can a man from Africa fit into your life plan? What about your calling?" Lilly questions.

"He's a physician and a business man who owns property in Ouagadougou and Kongoussi. He receives a meager salary from the government." Thea answers, ignoring the last question.

"He's the only one in the village with any experience in medicine. When his wife was killed he realized he had left behind a way of life he cherished. He returned to the village and built the clinic and ran it without any support from the government for several years."

A sprawling silence falls between them. They can hear the ticking of the timer, the drip from the kitchen tap, the tractor in the distance. Thea lets the clumsy silence lie.

Calmly, Lilly reaches for the map. Unspoken words remain between them. Leaning over the map of Washington together, they begin to plan their upcoming trip.

Lily lifts her head and says very quietly, "We'll come, you know, if you love and marry him," clearing the way for other conversation to resume. "Your father believes you know your own mind. I do too. You always have, and this is the most important decision you'll ever make," she says with a clear change of heart.

Overcome, Thea says, "In the beginning I'll have to translate everything for you, but I've been teaching him some English and he's driving to Ouagadougou to the American Embassy one evening a week to take a course. Mother, I think you'll see what I see: a prince of a man."

A fragile silence asserts itself again. Thea folds the map, having yellow highlighted their route. She embraces Lilly and retreats to her room. *They will come to Kongoussi,* she thinks. When she marries Augustin, they will come.

Standing on the tide gate above the dike, beyond the muddy trough of slough, listening to the quiet lapping of the river tide, Thea thinks of bringing Augustin to this favorite spot, suddenly knowing there are places too intimate to share. Thea watches the carp swimming lazily in the murky water like shadows of themselves, thinking thoughts that are only her own.

Next week after the hay is in the barn, after dear Ragna's funeral, they will travel to the World's Fair in Spokane, the first World's Fair to draw attention to the environment. Matt says it's overdue. She looks forward to less encumbered conversations.

They'll take the most scenic route through the northern Cascades, traveling on through the Okanogan mountains where her father packs in with the horses and mules to hunt in the fall of the year, where the streams run strong and meet their creeks and rivers downhill and sound like the distant clapping of a pleased crowd. The trout sometimes laze beneath the rocky ledges out of the current, and when they jump in the morning light they catch the florescent colors of the rain forest. Thea,

Lilly and Matt will bring home Red Delicious apples from Yakima Valley to eat and freestone peaches to can.

Thea is unable to bring Augustin fully to mind, unable to cast him in the role of a family member. She returns to the kitchen and mixes the corn bread for lunch, adding a little sugar the way she likes it.

After lunch she drives the new, yellow Case Caterpillar into the field, inhaling the freshly mown grass. The robust yearling steers trot along behind her and push against the gate after she goes through, but they stay shy of the single wire of the electric fence.

Her father has stopped his tractor. She drives up and cuts the motor to the Case. They sit side by side as they have so many times, on a horse, on a tractor, or in the turquoise GM pick-up. The cool breeze off the river rifles the oats still standing on the periphery of the field. The smell of the river and mown grass is at once sweet and crisp with a musty undertone.

Matt clears his throat as he often does when he has something to say. He resettles his Stetson hat and motions for her to climb on. As she leans against the fender, he drives up onto the dike to the furthest point of the property and stops the tractor near a rocky curve of the river where the Columbia's mild tides wash in and out. They stand on its banks, the fog drifting off the river like smoke rising from a languishing fire bed.

Long, straight timber have come loose from rafts towed by tugboats to the mill and are piled along the shore at all angles. A rusty chain coils around and beneath them. Some logs are bleached gray; others more recently washed ashore still have their shiny sap and the acne scars from being limbed.

Matt has built a cedar pole home out of such logs, a beautiful reflection of the environment, set apart by its open design. An expanse of plate glass frames the sunset where he sits in his brown, leather recliner. The hearth and chimney are of river rock from the Elochoman River. Few of the lines inside are broken except by treasured antiques.

Standing there together on rocky sand, Andy says, "Here's what our house is made of, stuff I could take without hurting the environment. I think it's a good way of looking at the world. I know you're struggling, trying to find resources for your inner self. I think we have the challenge and the responsibility to build a spiritual home from our own point of view, our own inner tabernacle out of the materials we have at hand, at the same time trying not to harm others' personal journey."

"I'm so confused by what's true anymore. After what I've seen in Africa, my whole belief system has fallen apart," Thea says. She leans to pick up a black flat stone, still wet from the tide and rubs its smoothness inside her vest pocket.

"Remember how the Israelites carried around the Ark of the Covenant in the wilderness? It's the same journey now, but a spiritual one. We carry about our own house of God through our own wilderness. We make our own rituals. Thea, use the resources available to you to build a spiritual home and find the peace only you have the ability to find. I have a ritual of coming here to the river with questions that have no answers. The full truth is not within our grasp."

Matt picks up a piece of driftwood, part of the root system of a tree sent upriver to the mill. "Lilly would like this in her flower bed."

"Daddy," reverting back to her childhood name for him, "I think I have started that journey. Not only am I questioning my faith and the path I chose, I love Augustin. I've told you that he's a Muslim and one of the Mossi tribe." Thea blurts out.

Matt clears his throat, "You probably realize I knew you came home for a reason, but I thought you just needed a rest. You've spent years to become an ordained minister, a world few women are admitted into. The doubts you experience are normal, universal. A man is lying who says he has the truth. Now, you want to give up all you've worked for?

"Are you telling me it has never been totally settled in your mind that Christ is the Savior of the world? Don't you understand how important that would be to me since I've planned my whole life around that one notion? Where have you been during the years I was in seminary? " She has never confronted either parent.

Thea's voice is urgent, "Kongoussi has changed me, but I believe I was open to that change. Your world can't be my world anymore, Dad. I can't duplicate what you've given me, a childhood where I never had to doubt that I was loved. I even believed I was *special* to God. You taught me our faith was the only way to God. I can't believe that any longer, nor, I now realize, do you. I don't belong in the ministry. I belong where I can make a difference in people's well-being. If I do affect someone's spirituality, it won't be intentionally, but by the grace of God."

"I can understand that you no longer believe in the same way, but Christianity has provided a framework and so much comfort and fellowship over the years. I've done a lot of giving back through the church. My own peace and deep fellowship have been the prizes."

"But don't you see? I bought into Christianity wholesale, not like you. I believed. I committed my life to becoming a minister and now I see the fallacy of believing there is only one way to God. I was only two when you were converted. I have a permanent soundtrack of church music going through my head. I just can't rectify what I've been taught with what I see."

"As I've said, I can't know the truth any more than you can, but the fellowship is rich.

Will you marry Augustin then, even though he's a Muslim from another culture? You've talked of him so often in your letters, your Mother and I wondered about your relationship. People generally talk about the one they love."

"He has heard much about you and Mother, as well," Thea answers, thinking of the predawn hours when she talked with Augustin of her family.

"We'll accept him if you do. There are many more chapters to your life. His questions will be just as large." Matt begins climbing the bank, trying not to disturb the bedrock of the dike. His back is straight, his jacket blowing in the breeze.

The biblical Jacob had to pretend to be his hairy brother Esau to receive a blessing from his father. She hasn't had to deceive. She thinks of the Shakespearean line from Merchant of Venice: *It is a wise father that knows his own child.* She has received blessings from both parents in one day. But it is her father who understands her unbelief and her ability to love an unbeliever.

Matt's voice quavers, "When we finish our work we'll drive east of the mountains to the World's Fair in Spokane, and pick up some peaches while we're at it. Tomorrow is Ragna's funeral.

FAREWELL RAGNA

The eastern light through the stained glass scatters shards of color over the hushed group of mourners. Lilly leans in, playing the organ softly, her head turned to watch as people quietly gather. Ragna's only son, John, in the second row, white headed himself, does not profess Christianity. He owns the often frequented grocery combined with a Chevron station on the old highway. He's well known for extending credit to people going through hard times, both for groceries and for gas. Residents who know him as well as Ragna attend from around the community: Puget Island, Elochoman Valley, Crown Zellerbach Family Camp, Beaver Creek, and Skamokawa and from the valleys of Grays River. The church is full.

Thea is asked by John to give a eulogy. She speaks as a long-time friend as well as a recipient of Ragna's skilled handiwork. Ragna's legacy of generous love was proven by her participation in rolling and sending the bandages, sewing the hand stitched baby quilts sent to her in Kongoussi. She could thread a needle by feel it seemed. Thea knows from Ragna's frequent letters she had lived up to her commitment to pray for her every day. The

Women's Missionary Council has now been named Ragna's Circle. Ragna will be missed; Thea tells those attending for her light heartedness and her ability to show love.

Pastor Jacobsen follows, seizing the opportunity to deliver a salvation message. "Like Paul, struck blind on the road to Damascus," he points out, "we often see more clearly when we are blinded by crises or loss. Take this moment of grief and loss to examine your own heart. How will you stand before the Eternal Judge?" More conciliatory he says, "The doors of the church are always open, 'whosoever will, may come.' Christ's blood was shed for you." Thea is sure he has John in mind. As a fisher of men, Pastor must believe that John would be a big fish. He casts the fly and reels it in instinctively as any good fisherman would do.

Lilly turns the worn pages of the hymnal, *Songs of Praise*, and resumes playing "Softly and tenderly, Jesus is calling" and people file by the ornate, open coffin and the abundance of predominantly white floral arrangements, for one last look. Thea and her parents have sent white lilies. The basket sits near the dark brown coffin, adorned with a spray of white roses, draped with a broad band of white ribbon. *Mother*, it reads. The Karan-Wemba was carved for such a funeral, Thea recalls. She will always keep it on a shelf in memory of Ragna.

The morning fog has not completely burned off, but patches of sunlight break through, promising a cloud-free afternoon. Headlights on, the cars of friends and acquaintances slowly follow the long black hearse up the hill to Greenwood Cemetery. At the graveside, John throws the first shovelful of dirt on the bronze coffin, a gash of sound followed by small rocks bouncing off. The casket is lowered without witnesses in bright sunlight after everyone leaves, and the fog has lifted.

A LETTER HOME

The following day, in route to Spokane, they travel north of Seattle taking the northern route through the Cascades, climbing the serpentine road carved among virgin timber until they reach the snowline where bare rock the color of newly laid asphalt is exposed in patches through the glistening, ice-crusted, shrinking snow. The jagged, saw-toothed mountains surrounding them are capped with snow, reminding Thea of the perched skull caps of the Elders.

They stop and follow a worn footpath along a ledge of a mountain, leading to a more expansive complex view of the slopes, crevices and the mountains ahead before the great valley. The colors vary from deep greens to the brights of saplings. Some of the mountains are in shade, some in shadow. One would need a full palette to capture the purples and charcoal blues, the darks, the lights of yellows and reds

Lilly, bundled in a blue down jacket, not looking like her petite self, carries their lunch in one of the round Mossi market baskets. Matt stands on a far ledge peering into his hunting binoculars, looking for eagles or an elk.

"The sandwiches are ham, leftover from what we took to the funeral dinner," Lilly says, handing a sandwich to Matt. He's reluctant to take it, having spotted a yearling buck with two velvety horns. He turns his back and continues to watch. Lilly replaces the sandwich. "Whenever you're ready," she says.

"But it's your bread I hope?" Thea asks fishing out a sandwich for herself. "Oh, and I see we have leftover apple cobbler."

Matt replaces the glasses in their black leather case around his neck and finds a place to sit. He looks to Lilly for his sandwich. "Where will we stay when we come to Upper Volta," Matt asks. "Is there a chance we could go on a safari out of Ghana? The animals must be magnificent."

"I think we could arrange for that. There are also guided Safaris organized out of Ouagadougou, but not like East Africa where you see a wider variety of animals."

Thea wants to capture this moment while they lunch, rather than talk to them leaning forward from the back seat. "But Dad, Mom, what shall I do about the prayer line I've told you about? I leave next week, and I don't know how to face my situation when I return. Many truly believe I can heal by praying for them."

Matt shifts his position on the projecting shelf of rock. "Have you thought of expanding the clinic that exists so people can be seen more quickly? Perhaps it could include midwifery, and girls like Rasmata could get help when they need it," Matt thinks aloud, slicing a Gravenstein with his penknife, asking Lilly for the salt and sprinkling it over each slice.

Before he finishes eating the apple, Lilly says, "You have the money your grandfather left you. How far would fifty thousand dollars go?"

"We can also help," Matt says.

They descend into the great, fertile Yakima Valley, where fifteen million years earlier molten lava flowed from fissures of the earth's crust, covering the area under thousands of feet of basalt, a tumbled, tangled blanket of rock. The Columbia Basin was formed by the fire and ice. Thea feels the fissures in her faith, flowing into a changing perspective, molten and dark like lava, forming new terrain. She takes her father's metaphor about a journey in the wilderness to heart and wonders how it can ever end, or if it must.

They drive north and east to Spokane, the second largest city in Washington State. Arriving, they see a changed city where expansive urban renewal has been done in preparation for the 1974 World's Fair. The exhibition features the clean-up of the Spokane River running through the city, making it visible. They cross the bridge over the green falls, admiring the changes along the rediscovered banks of the Spokane River. They attend the exhibits about the environment, trying to picture the calculated growth and impact of cities like Seattle and Portland.

They circle back through the Columbia Gorge, driving alongside the ripening orchards riding the crests of the hills, a green swath irrigated by the river.

That evening after a long sunset together with her parents, Thea retreats to her room and writes Augustin.

Dear Augustin,

Other than changing airports in Paris from Le Bourget to Charles de Gaulle everything has gone well. My parents were there, standing at the gate, to greet me and now we are doing a bit of traveling to some of my favorite places.

I only wish you were here or I there. The difference in place and the great distance magnify my longing for you. All the way here from Ouagadougou, during those long hours, I thought of us. You fulfill my dreams of being loved by a man, a man

such as you. You've touched the far reaches of my
being. I love loving you and being loved by you.

As you can imagine I see everything in a different
way; it's like having new eyes. The greens are greener,
the Columbia River seems wider. My home town
looks smaller and less alive. (I miss the sense of life
in Kongoussi.) My parents are changed somehow
too, in a rather indescribable way. Maybe I can
explain more after I've been here awhile longer
though time is growing short. They seem very in
touch with each other, and I feel a little like a visitor.
I wonder about everything seeming so different
since I've only been away these few months.

Just now you must be sleeping, or perhaps, you're
thinking of having me in your arms. Your gentle
spirit has invaded my soul. You've made me a captive
to your heart. Never was there such a willing captive!

I see differently with my spiritual eyes too. Augustin,
I even pray to your un-named, unknown God! I'm
still conscious of a continuous prayer ascending to a
higher power, but I feel reconciled to just BEING
and trusting without having to define or describe
God, let alone represent Him. After all the digging,
it seems I have hit rock and the water is less murky.
That inner place would not be changed to an inner
sanctum had I not come to Kongoussi and met you.

It comes to me that I've not written a love letter
before. But then, I've not loved before. I've reread
it and I'm hoping it doesn't sound corny. For so
long I kept myself apart, thinking I had a higher
calling. Now I think that was presumptuous,

*audacious really, to feel chosen by God. It
isn't just for your qualities that I love you, but
because you seem to have touched my soul and
I yours at a time when I felt truly humble.*

*Enough soul searching for now! Maybe someday
you can show me Paris. I've wanted to go since my
first year of high-school French. You must know
it well. When you tell me about it, I think of you
being immersed in a whole different world. It must
have been as difficult as it was wonderful. You said
it was Ophelia who called you back home after your
medical training. I'm glad to know you are suscep-
tible to the powers of love and that the love of one
woman is enough. I also know you wanted to affect
the level of health care available in La Haute Volta.
I imagine you learned a lot by practicing at the
Ouagadougou hospital before coming to Kongoussi.*

*I cherish this landscape where my parents put down
roots years ago when they left Kansas and their
families. I pulled out the old army saddle I had
at 12 and went riding in the forest the other day,
ducking branches and vines, so very conscious of the
contrast with Kongoussi. Remember when we took
Ibrahima home and how it seemed to me to be in a
vast wilderness? Here, Phoenix and I have to dodge
the bushes and still they brush against my legs. I
stopped among some clover beneath the shade of a
large cedar and sat on a moss-covered log. I let loose
the reins, and Phoenix nipped at the clover pulling
it up by the roots, nickering with satisfaction while I
sat there just thinking about leaving this land I love.*

Augustin, I wish you could feel the cool dampness on your face and hear the woods. There's music amongst the timber that you can only hear if you're very still. The whispering of trees, the dropping of a branch, a deer rising and leaving its thicket, the call of a bird and then the sudden rush when all the birds flutter from the tree at the same time. Here, you will never hear the silence of the desert. I remember the night we stopped and you had me listen. Remember how we listened for some sound? We heard total silence and experienced perfect darkness except for the stars. I remember the ground was still warm from the sun but the air was cool. You were there, and it was magical.

Anyway, I lifted the thick layer of moss off the red rotten log where I sat, subjecting hundreds of moving beetles to the light. I could have further changed their world had I scraped a fallen cone across the fallen tree. Even while replacing the moss, I knew I had disturbed their world for keeps. I felt a little godlike.

That brings a question to my mind. Are we God's created or just an inevitable result of cause and effect? Is there story of evolution never to be told in full? However we came about, I think we harbor in ourselves a constant hounding after a spiritual being we call God. I would rather believe than know. However, if we didn't need a god fashioned around our own fears and needs, I guess we could group them all together and have less conflict and more peace in the world.

There I go again with my unanswerable questions. They don't set me back as much as much as they pull me forward. I'm no longer consecrating

myself to the God I grew up with, but commit-
ting to doing well by my fellow inhabitants of
this mysterious and wonderful world. You know
the path well, seeing what you see every day.

My clothes aren't fitting so well. They're loose
now but I imagine I will come back a bit pudgy,
everything tastes so good. But being pudgy is a
sign of prosperity isn't it among the Mossis?

I was thinking about praying for the sick, me, the
yellow haired foreigner. When I was a girl I went
with my mother to what we called the old folks'
home here in my hometown. A few others came.
My mother played the piano, and we held a little
service for the residents. I think then my compassion
was more like condescension, the pseudo compassion
of the very naive. I think I pitied them without
seeing them as fully human. I didn't think of them
as real people, just the old and sick who seemed
useless and worn out. Sickness and old age seemed
like something that wouldn't ever happen to me. I
really dismissed them even though I was suppos-
edly ministering to them. It was condescension as
opposed to compassion. There's such a vast difference.

In Kongoussi, I felt something very different when
people started lining up at my door. The feelings came
from my stomach, an ache, wanting to change their
circumstances. You wouldn't think I would identify
with them, but nursing the babies and interacting
with their mothers changed me. I keep talking about
all this changing. I promise you the silt will settle,
and I'll be less pensive in the future. Right now I'm
in a doorway, on the threshold of a different life.

Je reviens.

Talato, your own

The following day they drive along the banks where the Columbia was never navigable except to Salmon even before the dams. Strands of young vineyards wrap the hills and plateaus like a cloth lain out in the sun.

Nearly home, they drive the last twenty miles on Ocean Beach Highway along the Columbia into the last of the evening light, a changing sky of violet and orange, striated with moving layers of gray and mauve cumulus clouds. The abstraction of the sky reflecting on the river ripples in the current, flowing west to the Pacific.

Thea and Lilly spend the next morning peeling and canning the freestone peaches, golden, soft, succulent, globes with stringy circles of orange and red around the pits. After the Kerr jars have had their hot water bath, Thea lifts the quarts out with gloves and places them in a glowing row on the cupboard As they cool, they listen for the pop of the lids, proof the peaches have sealed. They have saved back and plan to make a cobbler, Matt's favorite, maybe Thea's too.

"What a blessing," Lilly says, pleased with their result.

"Why for us and not someone else? Are we special to God?"

"I've never thought of it in that way."

"I hadn't either," Thea says, "Until I saw what it's like not to have God's blessing."

"You're questioning everything, then?"

"I have no choice."

Lilly responds, "I still feel as if I should be grateful."

"Gratitude and feeling special to God are two different things." Thea says.

The following day they follow Ocean Beach Highway to Long Beach, where they walk part of the fifty mile-long stretch of hardened, flat, wet sand. They walk in heavy mist on an average day, where hot and cold weather are as rare as the sunshine. They walk while the tide is stretched out, the waves in the distance invisible, the dark profiles of bent over clam diggers punctuating a foggy gray canvas. In the gauzy grayness with the ghost-like red and black of Matt's wool hunting jacket before her, Thea stomps on the sand and the breathing holes of the clams appear. She picks up a smooth shard of lavender shell and rubs it between her fingers inside her jacket. In the same pocket, she finds the black rock from the river. It will always remind her of her father's truthfulness.

Thea lets the wind buffet her, missing Augustin and thinking of bringing him here to walk with her in his broken but steady stride, experiencing the salt air and the enveloping sea fog for the first time.

Dockside in Ilwaco, inside The Duck café, they shed their jackets. Matt continues to stand until Thea and Lilly are seated. They order halibut fish and chips, expecting to savor the fresh catch from Alaska. The dark water beneath the wooden deck below them surges and slaps in its own rhythm against the pilings.

Thea looks ahead to Sunday, saying, "I'll be telling the congregation I am going back to live, and that I can't accept their support any longer."

Matt removes his reading glasses and rubs his forehead and chin in one motion. "Are you sure your life is there not here?" He reaches for his coffee and holds it to his lips, expecting a response.

Lilly searches for her handkerchief, nodding. "Your life will never be the same again," She says.

"I've lived under a canopy all my life, a canopy of love, for sure, and I don't regret it but I have to make my own life from here. I'm changed. I can't go back to the way I believed. You taught me to be strong and to stand for what I believe in. I'm twenty-seven years old. You've given me all you could."

"Do you know this Augustin well enough?" Lilly asks, patting dry her eyes. Her hair is limp from the wind and fog and no longer styled. She hardly looks herself.

A chirpy little waitress pours very hot coffee into their mugs without asking. She brings their fish and chips, and as they break apart the thick, white, steaming flesh of the Halibut, no one has the heart to continue discussing Thea's future. The juke box plays "The Way We Were," by Barbara Streisand. Thea has taken to heart their previous conversations, believing they will accept her choice. Nevertheless, they push back with questions.

They cross the Astoria-Megler Bridge, the longest continuous steel cantilever truss in North America, which spans the four miles between Megler, Washington and Astoria, Oregon at the mouth of the Columbia.

They drive to Cannon Beach and stay in a motel near Haystack Rock and eat Puget Sound oysters and Shelton, Washington clams for dinner in a narrow restaurant decorated with nets and transparent green Japanese floaters, rarities, collected from the shoreline. Thea feels the wonderful tiredness that only comes from being at the ocean.

In the morning, at low tide, they pick their way across the tide pools to reach Haystack Rock, a 235-foot high natural pillar, accessible from the beach. Thea stoops to search the tide pools to find a star fish among the sea anemones, crabs, chitons, limpets and sea slugs. She spies a pink one clinging to one of the wet, black rocks and points it out to Matt and Lilly. For the waves, they cannot hear each other. Terns and Puffins nest in the clefts of the giant stack of rocks. Seagulls pierce the air and swoop with the wind, stopping mid-flight to change course.

Lilly is chilled and returns to their rooms while Matt and Thea walk the beach, mounting the grassy dunes to catch a broader view of the pristine rocky coastline. Thea removes her old tennis shoes and walks into the cold surf. From the height of the dune, Matt takes off his sunglasses and smiles the smile that involves his whole face. His binoculars are looped around his neck, and he keeps a calloused hand on them. This trip is their gift to her. Perhaps they want the beauty and wonder of it to woo her back. "Where will you live, in Kongoussi or Ouagadougou?" He asks after stepping carefully down the dune.

"When we marry, Augustin plans to build a house in the village. We may just expand the one I'm in." Thea says.

"Can you grow vegetables?"

"Not easily, but you'd be interested to know I've transplanted a young mango tree for shade. When I bought it and put it in the ground it lost all of its leaves. The villagers thought it was dead. I did too, but Boukari continued to water it. The day it sprouted its first leaf, everyone in the prayer line filed by and marveled and said it was *Wennam Bosego*, God's blessing. Everyone seems to believe I have a special connection to God," Thea responded.

"Maybe you do. Jesus always touched the untouchables," Matt said referring to her morning ritual of praying for the sick, even the leprous. "We change whomever we touch and that's a miracle."

They had traveled in the fifties to Portland to a tent meeting where a sweating Oral Roberts, holding the echoing micro-phone closely, his voice low and husky, prayed for the sick. Sometimes the screeching feedback drowned his voice. "Where the healing waters flow," they sang. She remembers the long lines of people waiting in turn. The audience was told to hold the back of the metal folding chair in front of them as an act of faith while he prayed for a woman with a goiter. Thea held it, expecting something like the electric fence to pulse through it, but there was nothing. She stretched to see if the woman lost her goiter but they were too far away. She remembers feeling overwhelmed by the crowd, hanging on to her father's large, rough hand as they made their way out the green army tent's exit, her question about the miracle unresolved.

Thinking of the prayer line on her porch every day, she says, "Your idea about expanding the clinic is such a good one. I think *you* must have been inspired. I wonder what Augustin will think. The village is still adjusting to having medical care of any kind."

When they return to the motel, Lilly is sitting under her hair dryer in a pink plastic bonnet. She says hello over the noise, lifting the cap over one ear and returns to reading.

BEARING ARTIFACTS

On Sunday, Thea greets her many supporters, answering as many questions as she can before the service begins. On the altar, she displays an array of baskets and calabash covers she has shipped to Lilly. She is ushered to the platform and sits behind the podium alongside the Reverend Jacobsen. Sunday school classes have been dismissed and the children swarm about the artifacts.

Lilly plays the organ. Together with the pianist, Mary Valentine, they play an appropriate missionary song, "Bringing in the Sheaves." Thea thinks of the biblical Ruth who gathered sheaves from the edges of the fields, how she met and married Boaz though she was from a far country and a different culture.

"Ton Ba sen be arazana," she invokes. Our Father Who art in heaven, her voice breaks as she prays for daily bread, remembering the hungry Fulani and those in the village. Some of this congregation is suffering too but not as overtly, like Sheila, her friend, who struggles alone daily to fulfill her responsibility to her child. Though it is not a prayer, Thea continues in Moore with the 23rd Psalm. Her voice strengthens.

They sing "The Old Rugged Cross," and she thinks of her zandi, with its crooked poles, where no timber exists to compare to a cross. The cross on the wall behind her is of crude cedar planks from a tree Matt salvaged. When the planks came back from the mill, he dedicated them with a prayer in front of the congregation who had gathered around their barn and workshop. It was Easter, and he had made pancakes for all who came to the dedication. Out of the timbers he worked in the evenings and fashioned a cross for the new church.

The Mossi baskets are used to take a special offering on her behalf, and the members are generous. Matt is among the ushers, standing straight, one hand covering the other as he waits for the basket at the end of each row. Thea intends to give the offering to the Missionary Council in honor of Ragna.

Pastor Jacobsen is short legged and stout, his face wrinkled into a nearly perpetual smile or very quickly a scowl. His thick, gray hair dips to one side in a shiny wave. He keeps the front of his suit buttoned over his round belly. In front of the podium he keeps a stool where he stands while he preaches. Unlike Sidabé he does not leave the podium, but grips it with both hands.

Pastor Jacobsen introduces Thea as *their* missionary to Africa. She stands tall next to him even though he's on his stool. He asks for an ovation, and the congregation stands to give it. They are asked to praise God, and they do with upraised hands, some swaying in the Spirit. The profundity of the silence that follows causes Thea to wonder if God acknowledges those who seek with the distinction of His Presence no matter the creed, thereby validating one's faith in the contrived and various creeds. She remembers her sense of the All Powerful on the desert when she was in the depth of her doubtfulness. Maybe Jesus is a way but not the only way.

Thea gives her sermon. She describes the steadfast Sidabé, how he gave up trying to seat people in rows, how they sit now, legs folded, in a near circle. She tells of the congregation's

impromptu singing, the drums and tambourines and how difficult are the tunes of the French hymns. She speaks of the
importance of the early-on gift of the zandi from the Christians
in neighboring Kaya. She tells of the plans to build a church of
mud brick.

Changing course, going to the heart of what she wants
to say, she turns to Exodus and likens one's personal journey
through life to the time the Israelites spent in the desert. She
describes the extreme temperatures of the desert and talks of
the shelter one receives by believing in God, how the tribe of
Israel followed a cloud by day and a pillar of fire by night. She
tells of the tabernacle they wanted to build but couldn't, and
that instead they carried with them the artifacts, the altar and
the Ark of the Covenant, like our own artifacts of memories.
She describes their rituals and how important one's personal
practices are today to one's spiritual expression.

Inspired by her father, she describes the promised land of
Canaan, the land of milk and honey, the land the Israelites
couldn't enter. She compares one's life on earth to their journey
that is never completed. Our search for truth is never over, but
faith is required in its place. One finds peace while searching,
leaving some questions unanswered. Simply put, it's the journey
not the destination that matters. "We must invest in others,"
she emphasizes.

She pauses and thinks of her father standing at the end of
the property on the shore of the river, accepting in his spirit the
unknowable, saying it aloud to her like a confession.

She continues. Moses is recounted more than any other
prophet. His encounters with God are mystical. We should
expect and accept the mystical into our daily lives, revering a
God we cannot fully understand or know, expecting and trusting the promised land of peace will be ours in the end. She
draws on Kierkegaard whose work explores the emotions and
feelings of people faced with life choices. She speaks her heart

without mentioning sin and repentance or the need of a Savior. It is impossible for her to rule God out. She feels ruled by His Spirit as she talks.

Although it has only been five months into her tour, she tells them she can't hold to her first intentions. She can't be a recipient of their support. The congregation stirs. They turn to look at each other. Some shake their heads in disbelief. Some shed tears. Some are openly angry.

The day is rainy, overcast with a layer of low, gray, undefined clouds. Beside Pastor Jacobsen she stands at the door in the mildly cool air, embracing those in tears, giving what she senses is a final farewell. Some people avoid her entirely. Sheila stays behind, a question on her face. "I'll call," she motions.

Pastor Jacobsen comes to stand in front of her as the last few people leave, his face, anguished. He looks to her parents standing close by and takes both Thea's hands in his, pumping them, and says, "This can't be. This can't be."

Matt clears his throat. Thea looks to him, expecting him to interrupt. Lilly has gathered the Mossi baskets in her arms. She puts them on a pew and takes Matt's arm saying, "She's made her choice, a very difficult one." Thea isn't taken aback by her mother's defense of her. She slides to her side and the three of them are linked.

Thea confides to Pastor Jacobsen she will marry an African Muslim. "Then our investment is wasted," he gasps. He flexes up and down on his tiptoes. "People's faith in God will be lost because of your actions." He says with certainty.

"Pastor, I'm not responsible for anyone's faith but my own," Thea says. "I can only encourage others in their own faith and support them during their journey."

STORIES UNTOLD

The following day, the middle of the night for him, Augustin calls from Ouagadougou. "Talato, come home." He sounds distressed and alone and the connection is not clear. She wonders why he is in Ouagadougou in the middle of the night.

"I'm coming," she responds, reassuring him that she is on schedule. A conversation is impossible.

Thea goes to her room, draws the chintz, rose- patterned drapes and curls up with tightness in her chest. The time has been long since she has seen him. In her imagination she comforts him until he sleeps.

Unable to embrace or understand her irrefutable doubts about Christianity, she thinks of Descartes' *Passions of The Soul* on her shelf, when he says: "If you would be a real seeker after truth, it is necessary that at least once in your life you doubt, as far as possible, all things."

The calls and letters begin to come in after the sermon as the news spreads that Thea will remain in Africa to marry a Muslim. Geneva Olsen and Lena Pederson, two board members, co-sign a rancorous letter. Thea hands it to her mother. Lilly cries as she reads. Thea is surprised at the anger of lifelong friends. The phone rings, two long and a short, and they leave it unanswered rather than take the accusing, vitriolic calls.

Her high school classmates, those who might have understood, have left Cathlamet nearly a decade ago to build lives elsewhere; some are lost to the Viet Nam war. Neal, Reed, Joel or Becky would have welcomed a dialogue, judging from Thea's experience with them in high school --- especially during their senior year in current affairs class. Those who were college bound have not returned nor will they. The economy in Cathlamet is too weak. Needing a friend, Thea meets Sheila as often as her work allows, but they don't talk of Thea's choices. Thea grieves the dying of the community where she had thrived.

Pastor Jacobsen calls and contentiously asks Matt to resign from his position as chairman of the board. Thea is saddened. Later Lily and she see the tractor headed toward the end of the property, his sacred thinking place.

Knowing she is closing a chapter and that she won't be back in a long time, Thea begins to sort through her belongings. She selects her books: *The Heart of the Matter* by Graham Greene; *Little Women, Red Badge of Courage, Great Expectations, Grapes of Wrath, A Farewell to Arms,* others she can't leave behind.

She undertakes her walk-in closet, sorting through boxes one at a time. Most of her clothes can go to the Salvation Army in Longview. Her rusty skates go in the box of throwaways.

From a high shelf she comes upon a box, and realizes as she opens it that it is filled with her parents' private papers: their marriage license, the death certificates of their parents, mortgage papers on their first home, even pictures of them as children she has not seen.

She unseals an old manila envelope and finds a death certificate for a Sophia Lancaster, aged two years and two months, born in April of 1940, five years prior to her own birth and a year before her parents' move from Kansas. The cause of death: polio. She finds a single bronzed shoe. Thea peels back another layer and comes upon a photo nearly the size of the certificate. She pulls it close to her face: curly auburn hair like her mother, dark, snapping eyes crinkled into a smile like her father.

How can she reconcile moving to Kongoussi, now knowing she is their only child, choosing to live so far apart? Thea is not the name of a first born. Shakily she reinserts the certificate and replaces it. What is her responsibility to her parents? She grieves her own loss of a sister. She dials Sheila at work from the pink princess phone in her bedroom. She feels an unfamiliar separateness from her parents.

In the morning before meeting Sheila, she drives Lilly's Buick to Greenwood Cemetery and finds the grave, a small, granite angel shadowing a short plat. She brushes her hand across the shining dew-covered grass near the pale gray, weather-scarred statue and rakes off a few twigs. Alone in the morning's mist, kneeling in the shifting light she hears the wakening birds in the cedars and Fraser firs that encircle the cemetery. She guesses the timber was newly planted at about the age of the gravesite itself. She sees the tilted telltale tips of the Frasers, bent to the morning sun. She removes the wet leaves, and dark silhouettes remain on the stone. Thea traces the stains, the veins of the petals, with her finger.

Thea carefully removes a shriveled brown bouquet of what must have been pink roses and leaves a bouquet of multicolored dahlias from her mother's garden. The grave is well tended.

She hunches her shoulders and holds herself with both arms, shuddering briefly as she considers the loss of Sophia, Rasmata's death, the future absence of all she has known, even the beauty of the northwest. Because her parents held the secret of this little person, she feels betrayed by them and left outside their bond for each other. And yet she thinks they saw her as a replacement.

She feels a new kind of loneliness and an overwhelming need for Augustin, to be home, not here, but with him.

Thea meets Sheila for lunch at The Spar down on the deteriorating docks where they can count on a good basket of a cheese burger and fries. In the lingering fog, the smell of the creosote in the old pilings combines with the river's collection of detritus at low tide. The restaurant, with a dark paneled interior, has few customers save for some fishermen off the river. They are smoking, having a beer, and the shape of their conversation is ragged and weary-sounding..

Thea begins telling Sheila what she has found, "Think about the fact my parents have never told me. They've sheltered me from so many things. Think about what pain my leaving must bring them, to never really look forward to participating in my life or in my children's." Sheila and she are restored to their lifelong friendship.

"That's incredible. I suppose they *will* grieve your leaving more than if your sister hadn't died. It's like losing you too. But it isn't your responsibility to fulfill their dreams. It's your own that count." Sheila says.

"I thought at the time I decided to go to seminary and into the ministry after getting my master's, I would be fulfilling my dream as well as their own. I thought they would feel proud to have raised a child committed to God, someone active in the ministry.

Remember when Reverend Greenberg was here from the Congo and asked for people to commit their lives to the service of God? Remember how we were only six, and we both went down to the altar? Remember how he laid hands on us and prayed? I truly believed I was being called to Africa. I didn't imagine there was any other way to God than through Christ. Now I find my Dad has had doubts all along but wanted me to acknowledge God and have the friendships and fellowship a church would bring."

"It's a wound that won't heal. I don't go to church anymore. I only went on Sunday to hear you. When I needed help most, I felt judged and ostracized. I guess we're both in touch with a new reality now. It had to happen sooner or later." Sheila says, resigned to this rite of passage while grieving it. We sure spent a lot of time on those homemade pews."

"I don't regret the heritage I have. I'll always be influenced by it." Thea stresses.

"Everyone approved when you dated Mark."

"At least he was tall enough," Thea laughs, "Remember how I was taller than all the boys in our class? Augustin and I are the same height."

"Well, that's it then, it was meant to be." Sheila laughs.

"Sheila, I love him. I loved his hands the first time I saw them. They're remarkably capable hands . . . Besides, I love them touching me!"

After parting, Thea uses the steep planked walk to descend to the rotting, broken, floating dock and buys a Chinook Salmon for dinner.

The next morning, after breakfast, Lilly washes, and Thea dries. Another pot of coffee is percolating. Lilly stops momentarily and says to Thea, "You don't know this, but my parents didn't want me to marry your father. My father wanted to make the marriage contingent on your dad being a part of his sand and gravel business. Your father refused. I've never regretted my decision.

We left Kansas and came here and your dad worked in the shipyards during the war. My parents felt he had made a bad choice marrying me because he couldn't provide for me. That's why you never knew my parents. Both men were too proud to close the breach or cover the distance. My mother was killed in a car accident as you know, at age fifty seven, and I didn't see my father again until he was near death."

Lilly continues, "I blame the alcohol. Mama wrote about how it consumed him. He ended up leaving the business to his nephew, my cousin. Even though they were comfortable financially, mama was never happy. And then she died so young."

"I can see why you want me to make my own way, even though Africa is so far and so different. I understand that you feel you're losing me."

"There are more ways than one to lose people." She says, pausing. "Loss and life are conjoined. We'll come, you'll see, but make your own way, and do as you told me your father said. Build a home for your spirit to retreat and find refuge as life comes to you."

"We were also separated from your Dad's parents. He was born to your grandmother late in life, a change of life baby. They said we were too young. They were too poor to come to Washington by train and your grandfather never learned to drive. He was a drayer with a horse and a wagon. He never made the transition to an automobile. Nor did he learn to read or write. After he passed, your grandmother came to live with us. We saw most things differently. She was difficult."

"I remember Grandma being here. She was always so stern. If I have children, I don't want them to grow up without knowing their grandparents," Thea responds, touching her Mother's back and squeezing her shoulders.

"The church has been important to us, giving all of us a sense of a larger family and a place to develop and invest our talents. Bring them home, here." Lilly says.

THE FUTURE

Atop the stairs, she stands in the doorway of the plane, turning back to give one last wave. No one but her parents has come to Portland to see her off. They stand arm in arm. Matt takes off his hat and waves it. He's wearing his church clothes. As she looks back again, he has turned and is loosening his tie.

She looks down the aisle into the haze of cigarette smoke, blinking away tears. As the plane ascends and the snow-topped Mount Hood disappears, she turns to her book, trying pick up where she left off. She identifies with the young vicar who joins a tribe of American Indians in *I Heard the Owl Call My Name.* She doesn't get absorbed, nor does she engage the suited business man next to her.

Instead she recalls the recent hours on the tractor in the field with her father baling the hay, the rhythmic noise of the baler, the warm handles she uses to steer the Case. She sees herself step off to test the tautness of the twine. She slips a hand in to check for dampness. She sees an awkward newborn fawn in the underbrush of alders and points it out to her father who is ahead of her on the John Deere, raking into windrows the aromatic hay. The bales tumble behind her, and she feels the camaraderie with her father she felt as a teenager, the tender loss of it all.

In route to Paris, she sleeps on and off, stretching her legs from time to time. The flight is half full, and the meals are better on Air France. She remembers her parents waving goodbye at the airport and feels a slice of fear that she may never again experience the sheltering love she has had over the past month, over her life time really. When they're next together, someone else, a child or a husband will always be there.

Through the long hours she travels to Ouagadougou, toward Augustin, she captures more readily the memory of his lips, his touch, and the timbre of his voice. She turns his hand over and traces the brown lines on the light skin. In her mind, he pulls it back and touches her face.

The passengers blink and stir as the captain turns on the cabin lights and makes an announcement about the weather and descending altitude.

The Air France DC10 bounces as it lands, shuddering and braking hard on the short runway. The night air is hot and dry, and is sucked through the cabin as she disembarks.

A little dizzy, she holds firmly to the rail as she descends, watching her step in the inadequate lighting. People are streaming out to the plane. Among them is a tall, distinguished man with a pronounced limp. "Augustin," she breathes.

His arms extend toward her. She is home. Surrounded by people calling and meeting their expected passengers, he and Thea embrace. His hand goes up her back and she is drawn closer.

"Talato, my love."

"I'm home, Augustin. I'm home."

"My Talato, ma Cherie. Bien venue."

She searches his face and is reassured of her decision to be there with him. Her calling seems to be fulfilled or put away.

She is redeemed of it, no longer containing the burden of it. Her soul enters one of many sanctuaries she'll find in her long life.

They walk and she notices he uses a cane. It is polished ebony and the handle is in the shape of a lizard, arched and innocent. Still he keeps his hand behind her back. She doesn't put her arm around him in return. Not wanting him to feel supported, she draws his hand down into her own. She keeps his pace, which is swift and sure.

"Dr. Compaore has agreed to take my place at the clinic for several days. If you agree, you and I will stay at Hotel L' Independence.

"I've never thought to leave your side" she responds, knowing it to be true.

"We'll get our marriage license and you can get acquainted with Ouagadougou," Augustin says as they stand waiting for the luggage.

Having stood by until the last flight of the day, the gendarmes relax sitting slumped against the door posts, languidly smoking their pinched cigarettes, their guns within reach. Some have pulled their caps down over their eyes.

The hotel is modern, low slung with large windows. Stepping inside, it is cool and clean in contrast to the streets. Thea spends time in the hot spray of the shower shedding the stress of the long trip. Augustin waits with a white, hotel-furnished terry cloth robe. Chilled by the air conditioned room, she shivers, and pulls it snugly around her.

Late in the evening they sit at L'eau Vivre, a small, garden restaurant barely visible from the street. They're served by an order of Vietnamese Sisters, slender, young girls called to serve the church. They seem to be bowing even while walking gracefully to and from the kitchen, their slippers crunching on the gravel. They wear light brown, short, fitted habits. Dark brown wooden crosses on black twine dangle from their necks as they open and serve the bottled Vichy water. The smoking coils placed around the garden repel the mosquitoes. Jasmine climbing the nearby wall lends its fragrance.

She tells him of the plane stopping in Niamey, Mali where people boarded with chickens and small goats. "C'est L'Afrique," he laughs.

"The church is going up. I'm afraid your workmen have all abandoned your project of building a wall."

"Somehow I thought that was in the wind," She chuckles. "But tell me more. Why do you encourage the building?"

"Because of my own heritage and to honor your first intentions; because I see something good has come from you. These new Christians are sharing their grain, helping in the sorghum and grain fields. Most importantly, they're encouraging their children to go to school. Jean Paul tells me attendance is up and performance is higher. There are so many new students he is suggesting adding an hour to the day."

"The Christians are bringing their children to the clinic for immunizations. I have more patients than I can serve in one day. By the way, Norogo has become my right hand man, a good lab technician. I count on him to draw blood and test urine samples. He has much potential. Too bad he can't have a formal education."

Augustin continues describing new attitudes and the overall impact of the growing congregation. "The Christians are beginning to filter their water and are living more healthfully. They're relying less on the traditional ways of treating disease. After such a long season of drought, I don't know of any other way people could have been helped and encouraged more than through this little church. In fact, they seemed to be invigorated after you left. They've really outgrown the zandi. Now some sit under the sun to attend. Sidabé has changed the time to seven in the morning instead of nine.

Sidabé has stepped into your role, praying for the sick. Some believe they've experienced a miracle. Faith of any kind accounts for something, doesn't it? I believe anyone's faith can be honored, by God or man.

Sidabé has also begun to teach the members how to read in Moore, using the zandi and a blackboard. There are fifteen adults who have begun reading the New Testament. This way they can learn to read without learning French. We bought the Bibles and primers in the Protestant bookstore in Ouagadougou."

"We? Meaning you?" Thea smiles, tilting her head to one side, as does Augustin.

"My grandfather had his first taste of reading and learning as an adult after his conversion by the Weidman's. They came as early as 1914. Because of my grandfather, I have the education I have. As I said, I owe everything I am and have to my father and grandfather. They were true believers."

"Let's dedicate the new church to them if the other members agree," Thea says.

Thea orders a beef steak with a cream mushroom sauce. "Since when do you have such a big appetite?" he remarks.

"Remember, I came from a beef ranch," she laughs. Her memories co-mingle and Thea envisions him there out among the shorthorn cattle, astride the big Bay, Phoenix, Augustin and the horse all of one color. They trot together, Augustin alongside her father's horse, Amigo, a dappled gray Tennessee Walker. "When we go to America, we'll have to buy you a Stetson hat and cowboy boots." She can envision them together.

They walk past the metal, shuttered store fronts to the hotel, the lightest of breezes touching their faces. The streets are scattered with refuse from the market, and pieces of Le Monde newspaper used to wrap the peanuts skitter across the street. They don't seem to see anything but each other.

They hold each other under a wool blanket, one of the many sanctuaries she will find along her journey. They make love, and it is after as Augustin caresses her belly that he feels the slight mound of their child. On his elbow, he spreads his fingers across the swell as if to measure. She holds his hand against her. It is warm. Neither speaks. She turns into his chest. In the silence he pulls the blanket over her and reaches once more to touch her belly.

"Talato, ya Wennam Bosego," he says, holding her closer. It's God's blessing.

GLOSSARY

Baraka	Thanks
Baraka Wennam	Thank God
Beogo	Tomorrow
Bukkaru	Fulfulde for house or shelter
Djeli	One who sings at funerals
Dogo	House, home
Faan ya laafi	Everything is good, fine
Fulfulde	The language of the Fulani people
Fugu	Shirt
Gesebyam	Look there
Karen–Wemba	Belonging to God
Kourouga	Blowsy pants
Kongoussi	Name of the village which is the future tense of "to sleep"
Laafi bella	It's good, fine
Lorry	a truck, often carrying many passengers, their bags and animals
Mage	to heal
Mobili	Automobile
Moore	The language of the Mossi people
Nasara pinda	white healer
Ne pongo	Congratulations for having something new

Ne toumd nerei	Good work, to commend someone for good work
Norogo	rooster
Ouai	Exclamation point
Sidabé	Truth is
Useka	Thank you in Fulfulde
Wa ka ibeogo	Come here tomorrow
Wennam taas laafi	God give you a safe trip
Ya soma quai	It's good!
Ya Wennam bosego	It's God's blessing
Ya wousego quai	It's a lot with exclamnation point
Youki soda	An orange flavored carbonated beverge
Zandi	Thatched or grass shelter
Zecca	Pounded laterite floor

ACKNOWLEDGEMENTS

I wish to acknowledge the following friends and family, from which this book grew:

Dr. Robert Raleigh for his editorial sureness and encouragement;

To my daughters, Michal Lee, Talitha Lee and Dana Ramsey from whose hearts I delved;

And to my faithful friends who boosted my faith in myself: Charlene Comtois, Ian Dobson, Terri Littlejohn, Diana Lee, John Ballance, Pat Makos, Malcom Hodnett, and Inga Dube.

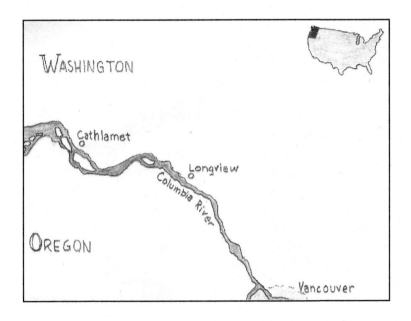

CPSIA information can be obtained at www.ICGtesting.com
Printed in the USA
BVOW08s1142120815

412963BV00003B/87/P